UNTISH WISHES

REBECCA PARCHA

UNTISH WISHES
A UNTISH NOVELLA

BY REBECCA PARCHA

NOTE FROM THE AUTHOR

UNTISH WISHES is a stand-alone novella set in the sophisticated, vampirical Untish world. While it can be read without any exposure to the Untish world, it is *best enjoyed* having previously read **Fangs of Fate** and **Daughter of Destiny,** as it plays with the content of each book, and is a nod to book three. Should you journey into the Wish World with Tate, Aether, and other beloved characters before having read the Untish Series, enjoy this introduction, and know that the full world and story awaits you.

Not all dreamers see the future, but some do.

CHAPTER 1
TATE

"**T**ATE, are you planning to stay out here all night?" Aether asked as his feet crunched across the pebbled beach.

I smiled at him and then focused on the waves once more as he moved behind me and wrapped his arms around my shoulders, holding me tightly.

"Maybe." I shrugged.

Being out here was better than in the palace with *all* the pestering questions and inquisitive eyes. Out here, it was just us. Me and my bonded. My mate. Together, we stared out at the deep blue sea. Its mesmerizing waves crashed against the stony beach before receding into the surf.

"I've always loved the ocean," I murmured, staring out at the expansive waters. Dragons soared far above in the distance, making their distinct colors hard to decipher.

"You don't say?" He gave me a playful pinch, and I jolted before smacking his arm.

"Smartass," I teased.

"As long as you're thinking about my ass."

I rolled my eyes as I laughed and leaned further into Aether's warmth, his chest cradling me from behind. With a rumble, he leaned down and nuzzled my head, eliciting delicious shivers.

I can elicit more than simple shivers if you wish, darling. His voice rumbled down our bond.

Oh...I know it, I responded in kind.

He tickled my side, and I squirmed in his arms, laughing as I did so.

"I surrender!" I squealed, and he finally relented, returning his hold to just around my waist, keeping me secure against his body.

With a deep, settling breath, I inhaled the warm, moist air.

It was so different here.

Back on Shappa, the air would be crisp, stinging as you inhaled, and certain parts of the Glenn would undoubtedly be frozen over in sheets of unforgiving ice. As much as I loved the sun and ocean, part of me longed for the harsh winter because it meant I'd be back home with Shae, Vala, and Ruby. The people we'd been forced to leave behind. The people we abandoned, even if we had no choice and were portaled here by my magic and connection to the crown...

I bit my lip and stifled the groan bubbling up my throat. Everything was messed up, complicated in unnecessary ways. A dragon bellowed from high above, releasing red flames that lit the now darkening sky.

A sky that was golden as the orange sun set—not red like in Shappa. The smooth surfaces of the pristine pebbles covering the beach reflected the late evening light; they weren't bathed in blood, charred remains, or embers. Here, we were safely secure in a cocoon, whereas everyone we left on Shappa was in danger, in the middle of a battle that we helped ignite before being spirited away.

Wrong. Wrong. Wrong.

The word repeated through my mind, and Aether moved his hands to massage my shoulders in an attempt to ward away the tension currently finding its home within my taut muscles. He manipulated the air, condensing it on certain pressure points, wielding the energy he so casually commanded with grace.

It worked. For a moment. And then the feeling of comfort evolved into guilt that sat squarely in my gut, sending bile rising up my tightening throat.

We were safely here, and they were there...with Chance and the creatures crafted from dark magic: the seethings, ghouls, and Tarragon. And that was to say nothing of the Head Chair and her vile ways. She was likely destroying the Embassy as we knew it—raising an army in the name of justice and sending soldiers to their deaths to fight for her twisted cause.

"You're shielding your thoughts, Tate. What's wrong?" Aether asked, sensing my inner turmoil. He sent a tendril through our bond, poking at the wall I'd commanded securely around my troubled mind.

"Nothing. Everything is fine." I released a deep breath and attempted to soak in the fragments of the setting sun's rays. I didn't need to bother Aether with these worries yet again. He'd had to listen to my vomiting guilt, anger, and confusion for hours on end, and for now, I just wanted to be near him. Even if that meant *I* was still a ship adrift in my inner turmoil, he didn't have to weather this storm with me too.

"I'd do anything to fix this for you, Tate. We'll get them back." Just like him to know what I was thinking and feeling without me having to say it.

I'm with you through all of this, his voice echoed inside my head via our bond.

I turned and met his gold-flecked, black eyes that intently looked at me with reverence I didn't deserve.

You can't get rid of me if you tried, he added.

I scrunched my nose and cupped his chin with my hand. A soft smile crossed his lips and lit his features. How I loved him.

Good. Because you're mine, I replied through the bond.

His eyes flared as his hands tightened around my waist. For a moment, I was suspended in his gaze until his eyes flicked up to above my head, and dread clawed its way through my heart at the reminder of *what* rested upon my head. I returned my gaze to the sea and rolled my shoulders back, attempting to loosen some of the building tension.

"I made you a promise. We'll figure this out." His voice rumbled with his breath hot on my neck.

"I know. It's just hard being here when they're there."

He nodded, remaining silent.

Together, we stood and watched the sun disappear into the sea. It was nearly too dark to see for a moment before the stars came alive, twinkling in their glory. The constellations here were different; however, a few appeared similar to those I saw back home on Shappa during the Winter Solstice. I used to map the sky with Fletcher and Irene over a cup of blood cocoa as we listened to the holiday music and cozied up under a thick winter blanket. The thought brought a pang of longing.

Things used to be so simple then.

Watching the stars dance in the sky, Aether asked, "Tell me, what do you wish?"

What did I wish for? More time with Fletch and Irene, my mom? To be with our family back on Shappa? For that childhood feeling of sweaters, a roaring fire, and family at the Winter Solstice. So many things that felt impossible.

"I wish—"

A flash flared across the sky as a star fell. The stony beach shook, and Aether's energy pulsed, forming a protective shield around us before the entire beach became washed in light that now engulfed everything.

In an even brighter flare, a ball of light roared through the sky, its trajectory aimed straight at our dome.

"Aether—"

The light hit the dome with a solid *thud!*

Aether's arms tightened around me, the ground suddenly evaporated, and together we fell. We became unembodied, immaterial, and light enveloped us; crystals floated all around our liquid forms, flashing memories of my childhood, Aether's life, and then scenes I'd never witnessed before. We were floating in a sea of diamonds, each one housing a different image. Just when I thought we'd be lost in this interim space, this feeling of incorporeal, my feet hit soft ground, and Aether's body became tangible around mine once more.

We were sitting and then fell awkwardly to the side, impacting ice-cold ground that didn't hurt, but instead moved to cradle our bodies.

We lay in a thick blanket of snow.

I pivoted and sat upright. All around were towering trees covered in white powder. I found my feet, even against Aether's protests, and began moving, staring at the forest in wonder. Each step sank six inches into white, frozen powder. Aether threw out his hand, willing flames to appear, but none came. He grunted as if trying to erect something, but nothing appeared.

"Tate, my magic…"

I blinked, looking for my internal pool of power, only to see an opaque door covering it. I tried to pry it free, to rip it off, and willed my power to flare, but…nothing happened.

"I can't access mine either." My tone was strained.

I searched for *her*, my inner dragon, but she wasn't in her normal pit of flames; in fact, there wasn't a pit of flames or power—there was a sense of nothingness, an empty void.

Panic clawed up my throat. I'd only just found my full self, and now I was locked away from her again?

"She's still there," Aether soothed, reaching out and rubbing my goose-pimpled arms. "It's okay. I can't access mine either, but I know he's there. You can sense her, right?"

I swallowed, forcing myself to focus. The empty void pulsed with something hidden. I searched internally and felt her presence hidden, remotely tucked away and obscured.

"Yes, I can feel her."

"Good. This," Aether gestured toward the snow surrounding us and the tall pine trees. "This has to be some bizarre dreamlike realm. Maybe this isn't real."

I looked at my hands and noted drops of liquid forming at my fingertips. White, fluffy ice crystals fluttered down around us, melting on my skin.

"I don't think so…"

"Tate, this *feels* off. Even without access to my magic, don't you sense something strange?"

I searched for any sense of wrongness. A certain sour note filled the air, but it was hidden in the crisp scent of pine and cinnamon.

"I sense *something*."

He nodded, jaw popping with the motion.

"What did you wish for?" he asked, looking at me intently.

"I didn't. I was just thinking of those I missed, of Shappa during the holidays, and…"

My eyes went large. "Oh, dear blood, did I send us here?"

"Wishes can sometimes be granted. But…I've never experienced anything like this. There is, however," he cleared his throat. "A Untish legend that one of the past monarchs of Mydant once made a wish, and it came true. He claimed he was transported to a fugue-like state where he battled his inner demons and saw the future. Not long after that, he prevented an internal war at Mydant, crediting his experience in the Wish World."

I swallowed. "At least that doesn't *all* sound bad. I'd love to see the future."

As soon as I spoke the phrase, the ground shuddered and shifted. I faltered, and Aether's steadying grip kept me upright until the quaking ground stilled. I shook out my left leg, annoyed once again at its shorter length. At least I transported us here with our current clothing, my augmented boots included.

In front of us stood a small cabin. It was cheery despite the oddity of this place. Smoke wafted from the chimney, and red, green, and blue lights graced its roof and porch rails. The cabin was composed of white and black painted wood, with a green wreath hung on the front door.

The distinct scent of mulled bloodwine and cinnamon wafted from the house, mingling with the crisp, pine-scented air.

An involuntary shiver shook my spine, willing my feet forward.

"Tate!" Aether's hand snaked out and gripped my arm. "Wait, we don't know what's inside."

"COME AND SEE!" a diaphanous voice boomed, and the cabin door opened.

We paused, and my eyes locked with Aether's. This place appeared gentle, but it was becoming clear that this was a web of delicately constructed lines.

"Should we—"

The ground violently shook. All behind us, the snow cracked as the ground and trees fell into a bottomless, black pit.

"GO!" Aether shouted as he grabbed my hand, and we ran toward the front porch. The ground behind us continued to vanish until about twenty feet out from the cabin, where the shaking stopped, and the snow-covered ground remained firm. We bounded up the steps away from the eerie, mystical forest, and burst into the cabin.

Stumbling inside, Aether slammed the door shut behind us, resting his heaving form against the solid wood. I bent over, bracing myself with one hand on a dresser as I took in my surroundings. A cozy fire with four stockings hung above it, roared from the center of the room. A tree graced with lights and strings of popcorn stood proudly in the corner, and a large couch sat in the middle, directly in front of the blazing fire. I paced over to the fireplace and ran my fingers over the soft, knitted stockings. Each one held a letter: 'A,' 'T,' 'C,' and 'S'.

Who lived here?

Before I could ask, Aether's lumbering form filled my peripheral as he bent over a basin of mulled wine. He leaned in and sniffed.

"If this is the Wish World, then some things are more than they appear. Some you *must* partake or participate in, and others are to be *avoided*. This," he leaned in and sniffed again. "Could be either."

I smirked at the look of distrust coating his features as he set the ladle down and paced over to the tree, examining it with suspicious eyes.

"What? Are you going to pull every red light from the tree? Perhaps tear off the blooddrop ornaments?" I teased. "Or maybe we should call forth St. Blood and investigate his sack of goodies first? Hmm? Make sure there's nothing nefarious inside his wrapped gifts?"

Aether ignored me and continued his inspection, turning to the stockings.

"'A'…for Aether," he murmured. "'T', for you my darling, Tate." His eyes squinted as he leaned in. "But 'C' and 'S'?"

I shrugged. "No idea."

"I don't like—"

The air in the room rippled, tearing and reforming as a portal opened, and two forms were thrown from it, landing on the lush red rug gracing the floor in front of Aether.

I stepped back, closer to Aether, and stared in disbelief at the two known faces staring up at me in shock.

CHAPTER 2

CHANCE

"CHANCE, I'm *not* sure. I've told you this before." Shae sighed heavily. "I don't know." She rolled her eyes as she wiggled her thin body further into the sofa, hot blood cocoa in hand.

"I think you do, and you're not telling me the whole truth." I locked my jaw, grip tightening on my spiked bloodnog.

We've had this fight over and over. Each time, I'd forgive her and move on, or I'd run away pissed. It didn't matter in the end—nothing did anymore.

"I know it's hard. I miss her, too. But...at least we have each other. You and Nora are the only family *I* have left. Can you please just trust me, believe me?"

I forced a tight, heavy breath out from my lips. "Fine. How's the blood cocoa? Is it hot enough?"

She snorted. "Nice diversion, *not!*"

"Well, it's something, yeah?" I took a swig of the bloodnog, savoring the aged whiskey mixed with the cream, complementing the nutmeg and iron aftertaste. "When will Nora be back?"

"Soon." Shae gulped her cocoa, leaving a red-brown ring above her lip. "And I promised her you wouldn't be any more trouble." She arched an accusing brow.

I ran my free hand over my face. I was tired. Tired of the anger living in my gut, tired of excuses, tired of the failed results. Even here in Shae's living room, exhaustion tolled. Red static danced across my body, the arm of the chair, and even around the glass of nog I held.

"What do you want from me, Shae? *She's* gone. Taken from me. Taken from *us*. She was the only good thing in my life, and she was stolen from me before I could make things right."

Shae's form stiffened as ice began to coat the leather armchair she was tucked into.

"I...I don't know, Chance. I miss her, too. It's heartbreaking, but—"

"But what?! *YOU* have Nora. You have everything, and I have *nothing*. I'm doing my best, why isn't that enough for you?"

"I LOST PEOPLE TOO, CHANCE!" She slammed the hot cocoa down, sending a generous splash across the wooden floor. "Tate was taken from me, too. She was like a sister, and now she's gone."

I scoffed. "Tate is the reason *my entire world* is gone."

Shae stood, and I found my feet, towering over my friend. We faced off for a moment before her hand reached out and gripped my arm, the very arm writhing in red sparks and vines of living lightning—an extension of myself and an expression of my inner turmoil.

"I miss her, too," Shae whispered. "With each passing day, I miss her and wish I'd been able to get to know her better. She had a soothing effect, and *I* think even Tate would have adored her. But we can't change the past; we have to move forward."

I growled as I thought about what transpired. Tate's actions, her power flaring, and the dragons that followed. No...there was no leaving the past behind.

There was revenge.

A flash occurred outside; the ground shuddered and then quieted.

"And Tate. She loved—"

"STOP SAYING THE BITCH'S NAME!" I snarled as my anger slipped its leash.

Shae ignored my shaking form, the lightning webbed across the wooden floor, and her grip tightened on my arm.

"Hey, I miss *them* both. I wish—"

Light flared and, as if solid, it crashed into the side of Shae's home before beams of light poured through the windows and swallowed us whole.

"Shae!" I cried, but my voice was lost.

I became intangible, not real, not right, not—

Diamonds surrounded us. Several held images of my *love*, my world with her honey-brown eyes and cropped brown hair; one depicted her with a smile plastered across her face, head tilted back in laughter. Others showed clips of her attacking seethings, being the badass she truly was. And still some were more intimate. I reached for one that showed *her* smiling and cupped the diamond briefly in my hand.

How I missed her.

I would've made things right.

I would've given her everything.

And that hope, that redemption and future, was stripped from me by a mahogany-eyed, magic-harboring bitch.

The diamond flared at the thought and then crumpled into a million shards of diamond dust in my palm. Fate herself must hate me.

The world began to spin again, compress, and then expand. A shimmering shape appeared in front of me before an unknown force shoved me toward the shimmer.

I was falling and then...I wasn't. My face smacked a thick, red rug. Shae *oofed* next to me as her body crashed into mine. Startled, I shook my head and forced my eyes to focus. A tree draped in corded red lights was just ahead and to my side...

Two forms towered over me.

Two people I never wanted to see again.

And yet, the same two people I'd been hunting.

Tate and Mardi.

CHAPTER 3

AETHER

"**A**ETHER, calm down!" Tate grabbed my arm, stopping me mid-lurch. Instinctively, I reached for my power, willing the energy around Chance to freeze him, or better yet, strangle him. Nothing came because we were in the damned Wish World, where I was rendered powerless.

"No," I growled. I reached for my non-existent sword, cursing when I realized I wasn't even armed.

Chance jumped to his feet and extended his hands at me, snarling like a large dog, and then looked at each hand, panic lining his manic eyes.

"It doesn't work here," Tate spoke calmly, and Shae rushed into her arms. "Oof!" Tate took a step back from Shae's impact. "Shae! I missed you so much."

"Girl, me too! I was actually just talking about you and then..."

Tate pushed Shae back and looked into her blue-grey eyes. "I was thinking about you too, and then a flash occurred, I think a star fell and—"

Tate's eyes snapped to mine.

"Aether. You said we're in the Wish World. Do you think my wish brought them here?"

I snarled at the thought of her *wishing* for that piece of vampirical shit standing in front of me. "Possibly."

My jaw locked, and I took a protective step in front of Tate and Shae, challenging Chance, who began pacing like a caged animal.

"Fuck!" he screamed and pulled at his long-curled hair. "Tate. You KILLED HER!" He rushed toward Tate, and I intercepted him, tucked my leg behind his, and pushed, sending us both tumbling to the ground.

"Aether!"

"Chance!"

Tate and Shae's voices screamed for us to stop and behave, but fuck that.

"Fuck YOU!" I shouted at Chance as we rolled on the ground.

He was fast, skilled, but I was bigger, older, and more importantly, stronger. I pinned him to the ground and bared my fangs as I snarled at him. He thrashed beneath me.

He screamed. "Go ahead. End it!" Chance threw his head back, exposing his neck. I sensed the blood coursing through his soiled veins. It'd be disgusting, but I'd rip out his throat.

"Aether, no." Tate placed a hand on my back. "Don't."

Why shouldn't I? "He's a threat to you. If I don't end him, he'll end you."

"He's right," Chance croaked. "I can't wait to tear your head from your fucking body! It's your fault!"

Tate flinched next to me. "Chance, I'm so sorry. I tried to save her, I really did, but she wouldn't stay inside the shield and—"

"LIES!" Chance's voice rose, and I pressed my forearm to his throat.

"Even this asshole's—" he gulped as he strained against the pressure I applied to his neck. "—name isn't Mardi, is it? You're all liars."

Tate exhaled next to me and looked at her feet as she bit her lip. I didn't need the bond to know Chance was manipulating her emotions, playing with the guilt she carried. How dare this piece of shit make her feel that way?

Moved by that thought alone, I leaned in and revealed the full length of my fangs, preparing to strike.

Ice.

Ice swelled around my body, pulled my hands from his arms, and coiled around my neck in a frozen whip, tugging my head backwards.

"Shae, what the hell!" Tate exclaimed as she dropped to her knees and pulled me into a protective hug.

"I...I don't know why, but apparently *I* can still wield." Shae's voice quivered. "Blood knows why. I never wanted powers," she murmured even as she willed her magic to move my body away from Chance, who she also actively restrained. "But given that I'm the only one who can apparently wield, you boys WILL behave. I'm going to make sure of it."

"Shae! END HIM! *They're* responsible for killing my *love*," Chance spoke, and moisture formed in his eyes. If I didn't hate him so much, I might actually feel for him. Too bad I loathed every fucking thing about the male.

"Chance," Shae spoke, side-stepping Tate and me, until she knelt beside him. "I know you're hurting. And what happened was horrific. But we're the ones here now, and I know *she* wouldn't want us fighting. She wanted Tate to save you. She cared for her too, I saw it with my own eyes on that final day."

Chance just snarled but kept his lips shut even as his fingers dug into the rug, attempting to shred it. Too bad for him, vampires didn't have long claws.

"Things are messy, complicated, but *this*," Shae gestured to the cabin and us, "isn't our reality. I agree with them; this is the Wish World, and I don't know what that means for real life, but I'm not going to let anyone get harmed. Not as long as I can stop it." Resolve straightened her back.

"Shae's right, Aether. No harming anyone here. Okay?" Tate nestled her head against my shoulder as her body hugged mine from behind.

I gritted my teeth. I wanted nothing more than to destroy the male who threatened my bonded. And yet...if Shae could keep him under control here, and Tate asked me to grant him mercy while in this realm, I could try. Would try. For all I knew, this was a weird test, and they weren't really here. Tate needed to pass this test, and I'd do anything for her...including swallowing my rage. For now.

"Fine," I gritted out.

"Fuck you all!" Chance shouted, but then the icy manacles at his wrists dug in deeper, and he keened.

"Chance, this isn't even real. Please, behave?" Shae asked. Her lips turned a deep royal blue as she spoke, and her eyes haloed in living rivers of ice.

Chance merely nodded 'yes' and grunted. That apparently was enough for Shae as she released both of us, and I found my feet, squaring off against him, prepared for his inevitable snake-like strike. I wouldn't start it, but I'd be damned if he hurt Tate.

"Good. See, I think we can all coexist." Shae nodded to herself.

Tate licked her lips next to me, and then fixed a determined gaze upon the sorry excuse of a male. "Chance, I do want to say I'm truly so sorry for your loss. H—"

Chance stormed her, and I stepped in his path, ready to throw another punch.

"Don't you *dare* speak her name. You're trash and have no merit. I will not have her name sullied by coming out of your cunt mouth—"

My fist connected with his jaw, sending him flying backwards. I lunged and then pounded his face again with my right hook.

Ice wrapped around both of our legs and yanked us apart, then froze us both where we stood.

Shae heaved. "Well, that lasted long."

"Maybe we should just let them cool off." Tate sniffed.

I longed for our bond, to feel what she felt, to mind-talk with her.

I loathed this realm.

The room shook violently, and then three holes tore through the air, shimmering and pulsing, before vanishing and leaving three tall, ominous doors in their wake.

Two of the hulking frames were dark, opaque, and uninteresting. But the one on the far left lit up and pulsed a vibrant light. Music began streaming through the door, wafting through the room, encircling us.

"That tune…" Tate began, eyes becoming haunted.

Chance exhaled deeply, and even Shae appeared to be shaken.

"What?" The ice holding me back vanished, and I moved to pull Tate into my arms. "What's wrong?"

Her eyes misted over. "It's the Winter Solstice song my mom—" She swallowed. "Irene would sing to me."

Understanding flooded my mind, and I pulled her in tighter, giving her the secure embrace I could.

"We have to go through." Shae nodded to the door.

Tate moved from my arms, but my hand caught her wrist. "Wait."

I leveled a look at everyone, Chance included. For once, he didn't reek 'asshole' but appeared to be actually shaken.

"This is the Wish World. My understanding of it is that there are *tests*. They'll be personalized to each of the dreamers, the wishers. Whoever it is will have to face their inner demons. We *can* get harmed here. The ruler who returned from the Wish World was full of stories about *other* wishers who didn't overcome and instead succumbed to a fractured mind. So, tread lightly, act valiantly, and be smart."

I swallowed, hand tightening on Tate's wrist. I hated warning Chance; he didn't deserve it. But this could be a test for Tate, and in that, a test for me. Warning all of us was the safest way to pass whatever lay ahead and to ensure the best chance for Tate's success in the impending trials, along with her safety thereafter.

"Aether, we *will* be okay." Tate turned and cupped my cheek before standing on her tiptoes to give me a kiss. I melted into her softness but then stiffened.

I had to remain vigilant. Alert.

"Who goes first?" Shae's voice drew my attention from Tate's mahogany eyes to the other two people in the room.

The door pulsed, and the floor around us began to vibrate. The mantle holding the stockings flared, and the one with the 'T' and 'C' began to hum.

Destiny had spoken.

The floorboards shook violently before being torn into a black pit that was swallowing the room whole. The festive tree fell, plummeting into darkness, becoming smaller and smaller until its lights were no longer discernible.

"Now!" I shouted, and grabbing Tate's hand, we stepped through the door together.

CHAPTER 4
TATE

"TATE?" Aether's voice reached me. I blinked several times as my eyes adjusted to the scene around me.

A fire lit in *pink* flames roared from an oversized hearth in the large living room. Even with its tall walls and sparse furniture, it felt cozy. A tree in the corner—at least twelve feet tall—was adorned with pink lights and ornaments depicting dragons, crowns, and various figurines. It was grand, but also homey—right.

A woman with mahogany eyes and *my* nose stood, cradling her baby by the fire.

"Isn't she perfect?" she said, staring at the baby, swaddled in fine linen.

Inexplicable tears welled in my eyes, and Aether moved his hand to caress my arm in comfort as I stared at the female. Her golden hair was piled in a messy bun atop her head, and the gown she wore, while elegant, was simple with no added pomp.

I liked her immediately.

A male with a blurry face, one I couldn't make out, moved to stand beside her.

"She's your spitting image. Pure perfection." He lifted his finger to the swaddled babe. A tiny hand reached up through an opening in the linen and gripped his index finger. The man smiled broadly and looked at the woman. "Look at that! She likes me."

The mother's melodic laugh surrounded us.

I moved, drawn to the happy family, and peered over her shoulder. Even from a foot away, her warmth reached me. Aether stepped closer to me, feet pounding the solid ground, as he offered solidary comfort. I glanced at him and noted emotion filling his eyes.

"I just worry. What if, what if she's not alright? What if we didn't birth her in time, and the toxin reached her, hurt her quicker than we thought—"

"Shhh," the male soothed, lifting the woman's chin to meet his eyes. "The Luner doctor said she's healthy and sensed no lingering magic. And if she's wrong, if she missed something, we'll handle it together—as we always have."

She swallowed, tears slipping down her face, and the baby cried. Both of their attention snapped to the wee babe.

I reached out for the woman, but in a whisp of smoke, they both vanished. I stared at the spot where they'd stood. I'd been so close to them, so close to touching and holding them...to the encounter I wanted more than anything.

"Tate, this is the Wish World...it can be cruel. I'm sorry." Aether grabbed my hand gently and gave it a squeeze. "We have to be careful—"

Cries sounded from outside and overpowered my senses. They were in trouble. I ran, following the screams, through the grand foyer with its ornate banners, through the grand double doors, and out into the garden. A garden I knew.

The hidden castle's garden.

Only, this time, instead of immaculately upkept flowers, they were shredded. Fire lit the sky in red and pink streaks, and a woman's scream sounded. I rushed toward the wails, the cries, just in time to see the woman on her knees, clutching her stomach as blood seeped from her lips.

"NO!" I screamed, and my feet pounded the cobblestone path until I hit what felt like an invisible wall. I willed my feet forward, but no matter how fast I ran, I made no progress—I was suspended in place.

"Tate, this may be a test. We need to be cautious." Aether's hand gripped my arm, urging me to remain calm.

"She's my MOM." My voice broke as I spoke, and I tore my arm from his embrace, pushing more will into my movement, frantic to help the female who birthed me.

The same unknown man from the living room knelt beside her. He wrapped his arms around her and rocked, before lifting his head to the sky and screaming. His loss and grief were palpable.

The world shook, and a figure dropped out of the sky. She landed, wrapped in red flames, and stared at my mother cruelly.

Something about her seemed familiar, like I should know who she was, but the harder I tried to decipher it, the sharper the pain in my skull became.

"Save yourself!" my mother cried, squeezing the male's arm and then shoving him backward. "I'm begging you. *She's* going to need one of us!"

I froze watching the scene unfold.

The woman coiled in red flames stalked toward them, lifting her hands as she laughed, and the very air soiled from her screeching sound. Her breath sent a ripple of tainted vapor that killed any living plants the moment it touched them.

"I can't." The male shook his head as he leaned into my mother.

"You must," she spoke and cupped his cheek. He bent down and kissed her, even as her blood force drained, and then she shoved him back.

"Go. Survive for *her,* our daughter! GO NOW!" she commanded.

The male, my father, reluctantly tore himself from her and his face filled with resolve.

In a blurry blink of white, he vanished.

The vile woman in red approached my mother who was crumpled on the ground. "You think that will stop me from hunting her?

Extinguishing your little flame?" She laughed hysterically. "Stupid bitch."

My mother found her feet, still clutching her stomach with one hand, and then snarled at the approaching threat. "Poor cousin. Always seeking what you can't have."

The woman in red snarled and sent a flash of red flames toward my brave mother.

"NO!" I screamed, running toward her, and this time, I moved. I pounded the cobblestone path, Aether on my heels, as I desperately approached her.

My mother threw out both hands, and a wall of pink flames blocked the violator's path. She looked at me over her shoulder, sadness in her eyes. "Look at you, my dear girl."

"Mom," I whimpered as I reached her, stopping a foot away. Blood still dripped from her mouth, and with the force she exerted, it also began to pour from her eyes.

"You've bloomed as I knew you would. Be fierce, be on guard, and ESCAPE! I'll hold her off." She choked on blood at the end.

"No! Let me help you!" I pulled on my magic only to find there was none.

She smiled at me, tears mingling with the blood. "Do this for me, my girl. Survive."

Aether stiffened next to me. "Tate, I think we need to go. That's the test."

No. I couldn't; I'd only just gotten here. I'd only just spoken with my mother, even if she was just a version of the real person in this Wish World, how could I abandon her?

The woman in red's wild laugh breached the flames. "Stupid girl. Of course you'll abandon her, just as she abandoned you!"

Her voice seared me, sending spiking pain down my back. Recognition dawned but I was unable to speak her name, even as hate anew blossomed in my gut.

"I never left you willingly, Tatealia. My life drained, and I had to say goodbye, for now. But here, now? Let me do this. You must run. You must escape. FIND THE DOOR. GO NOW!"

As she commanded the last few words, energy wrapped around my legs and ignited.

Tall, red stalagmites shot through the ground, piercing the garden in random attacks. The sky filled with ghouls flying above, and my mother dropped to her knees as she screamed. She poured more of herself into the wall of flames even as her body began to disappear.

No!

"MOTHER!" I screamed as I reached for her receding form. For the briefest moment, my hand touched her warm skin and jolted a memory.

I needed to flee.

I had to keep my mind intact.

"Tate!" Aether shouted as he lunged out of the way from a stalagmite tearing through the cobblestones. It broke a tree branch free, and Aether reached for it, preparing to wield it like a club.

My mother vanished. The wall of pink flames flickered but remained.

"Run if you must, Tate. But I'LL FIND YOU!" the vile woman cooed, her voice turning into a lunatic's howl.

I stood, looking for a weapon, as a ghoul dropped in front of us, landing in a crouch. It tucked its white wings back against its milky, red-veined body and snarled—loosening black goo that dripped from its unhinged mouth.

A melody began playing from above, the same one Irene had sung to me as a child. The Winter Solstice tree song. In the background, a giant ticking sounded, methodic, as if a metronome or a...

"Clock. Tate, this is our test. We have to get out of here in time."

"Let's find the door." I picked up a broken stone from the wall and hurled it at the approaching ghoul. To my surprise, it hit its mark, and the ghoul blinked and then vanished.

"Okay..." Aether shook his head. "Where to?"

"Why are you asking me?!" Panic sank its claws into my tenderized heart.

"This is a test meant for you. Which means, only you know the way to the door." Aether's face filled with sympathy before flashing to panic as he raised his club and struck a ghoul behind my back. Like the other, it flashed and then vanished.

I surveyed the yard. The stalagmites blocked several paths, but there were three open options. Ghouls began to gather by the dozens, surrounding us, blocking the far-right exit. That must be the way.

"Let's go!" I shouted as I picked up a handful of pebbles and began chucking them toward the approaching ghouls. Several hit their marks, and from the briefest brush of them, the ghouls flickered and then disappeared.

Aether lifted his club and began swinging it wildly at the beasts, taking one after another down. Three landed ahead of us and outstretched their hands, releasing an onset of red flames.

"Duck!" I shouted as I rolled to the left out of the way. I crawled behind an erected red stone jutting out from the ground, twenty feet high. I needed more rocks. Searching, I leaned around the stalagmite and placed my hand on it—*zap!*

A scream escaped me, and Aether's grunts increased as he shouted my name.

I pulled back my hand to note blisters dotting my skin, oozing pus. Poison.

"Don't touch the stalagmites!" I screamed as I cradled my hand and moved toward Aether, who struck the last ghoul down, a branch landing in the beast's head.

"What happened?!" he demanded as he searched the sky for the next target before glancing at my hand. "Fuck, that looks bad, Tate."

"I'm fine." As I spoke, a dinging sounded above, a click gonging as the song began to hit its crescendo.

Ghouls landed behind us, in front of us, and the vile woman's screams sounded as a wall of red flames swallowed the garden behind us. As the heatwave approached, my skin warmed and the blisters boiled.

"Tate..." Aether readied his club.

I pivoted, doing a three-sixty, before I felt a pull. I gripped Aether's forearm, tugging him with me, as I ran around stalagmites. The flames licked at our backs, incinerating the ghouls, and getting precariously close. A few ghouls dropped in front of us and I kicked the closest one, delighting when it howled as its life flickered away. We ran faster, avoiding the fresh stalagmites tearing through the ground. One caught Aether's shoulder and he shouted as blisters began forming and spreading, pus leaking from each one.

"Just a little further!" I shouted as we dodged the rising stalagmites and attempted to outrun the liquid flames chasing us.

The gong sounded again, the strike of nine.

The song's melody hit the first note of the last chorus.

A flash occurred, and then a tearing in the air, a shimmering, and a giant door dropped. The portal. Its frame flared in violent red, and a gold shimmer poured from inside its opening.

"There!" I shouted as I pulled Aether with me.

Just as we approached the door, the ground shuddered, and a giant gate erupted from the land, covered in crisscrossed vines that made a web; each vine held various red rocks and stretched ten feet wide across the opening, at least five feet deep. It pulsed a certain wrongness along with poison that leaked from its leaves, vines, and rocks.

The melody began its outro and the gong struck eleven.

Screams erupted behind us as the liquid flames hit my back, melting the clothes from my skin.

Aether squeezed my hands but looked at me with trust. It was now or never.

As one, we tore through the web, screaming in agony as each poisoned vine and barb nipped at our flesh until we hit the portal and *boom!*

We were tumbling, Aether's hand in mine, through a world of darkness before abruptly falling onto a hard, wooden floor.

I braced my hands on my knees, searching for Aether. He was already standing, back straightened, ready. We were in the cabin; its fire roared calmly as if nothing had occurred. I turned to see the door flash, and red hulking eyes staring at us with loathing. With a final scream and flare of her eyes, the portal closed.

"Are you alright?" Aether cupped my face in both hands as he searched me.

"Fine. I think." I looked at my hand, searching for the injury, but no blisters were found. No poison. My arms were as unscathed as my legs. The injuries had vanished. "You?" I asked, searching him in turn.

He didn't have a scratch on him.

"Aether, that was so strange."

His jaw locked, but he simply nodded before pulling me into a hug. "The Wish World can be harsh. Granting you a glimpse of what you desire and then making you pay."

Tears began to slip from my eyes as I stared at the fireplace lit in orange-yellow flames. The stocking above it, the one with a 'T' had halfway disappeared, nearly gone. My eyes traced the other stockings, noting the one with a 'C' actively shuddered.

"Aether, where are Chance and Shae?"

CHAPTER 5

CHANCE

"CHANCE, where are we?" Shae asked as she stood, brushing sweaty hands on her pants.

"Not sure." I surveyed the room. It appeared to be a guaramen's office. Immaculately upkept books lined the shelves in the corner, and a large oak desk stood in front.

"Do you remember this place?" Shae spoke as she moved and picked up a portrait that graced the otherwise unadorned desk. She snorted as she extended it to me. There, in the ruby-studded frame, was a photo of my father.

Nausea rose along with guilt, and both warred inside my throat. He was gone. Part of me was relieved he wasn't here to pass judgment anymore, but the other part also missed him.

Oh, irony of ironies.

"I don't, but...it appears standard issue." I inhaled the sour scent of my father's cologne. If this were his desk, it'd be only too on-brand for him to boast a photo of himself on *his* desk. A dry snort escaped my lips.

In the corner of the room, a depressing, small tree sat on a table, wrapped in red lights with a vase of bloodwine beside it that rivaled its size. Just like old times.

Voices accompanied by footsteps echoed from the hallway beyond. My back straightened, and I sidestepped closer to Shae, whose fingers were coated in frost.

"I'm sure you're an outstanding fighter, but if you wish to be *more* than a grunt-level arche, you need to prove yourself, Miss Holland," a voice boomed, and my insides quaked.

The large door to the office tore open, and a husky frame stalked through: my father. I ignored his disappointed gaze and looked at the small frame behind him: Holland.

My Holland.

Tears filled my eyes as I stood frozen, unable to move or speak.

"Of course, it'd be my honor. I will prove myself," she spoke, tipping her beautiful head upwards. Her brown hair was longer than I recalled, past her shoulders, but her honeyed eyes were just the same. Smart, knowing, determined, unwavering, even in my father's critical gaze.

He paced over to the bloodwine and filled a large stem for himself before pivoting to face her once more. "Yes, see, I'm told you have Emo Tasting as an ability. But it's more than that, isn't it?" He arched a brow as he sipped.

Holland swallowed and bit her lip nervously.

My father extended a hand to ease her visible discomfort. "No worries. Compulsion is a gift, Arche Holland. I understand why you hid it, and that dishonesty shows you have the backbone needed for Dux. So do you?"

"Sir?" Holland tilted her head in the typical way she would when she was deep in thought or confused.

I stepped closer to her, noting the unshed tears lining Shae's eyes as she too watched Holland. I moved close enough to touch Holland, but she looked right past me at my father, oblivious of me.

"Do you have the backbone for compulsion and secrecy?" my father asked, tapping his cane as he approached her.

"Yes, sir. I do." She nodded her head once in confirmation, confidence straightening her back.

"Well then, welcome to leadership, *Dux Holland*." My father patted her back before turning once more to look out the window that oversaw the entire Western Outpost. Trees towered in the distance along with stacked, dismal barracks.

This must be my father's Western Outpost office.

Things began to click into place. This is where Holland, my dear, sweet, brave Holland became a Dux. This is where she trained.

This was her story.

"Thank you, sir. I won't let you down."

"Very well. Go see Anax Drew, he'll get you set up." My father waved her off.

Holland's eyes filled with excitement as she bowed respectfully to his back before stalking out of the office. Like a string controlled me, I followed her, awe filling my heart.

Even the way she walked was soothing.

Holland.

My Holland.

My everything.

I swallowed as Shae's steps sounded beside me as we trailed Holland through various hallways, and I savored the bursts of her scent that filled my nostrils.

She entered an office and then stood, back straight at a desk. A weasel-like arche looked up and snarled at her. "Appointment only."

"I was sent here by President Dale," she spoke confidently.

The weasel narrowed his eyes at her.

Waves of energy flowed from Holland and struck the arche, whose jaw slackened before he pressed a button, and the adjoining door popped open.

"Thank you, I appreciate your cooperation." She winked at the arche, who still remained shaken, eyes holding no intelligible signs. As we followed Holland into the office, I leaned over the desk and slapped the scrawny male. To my delight, I made contact with his pasty skin, and he rocked back in his chair—ever the dumbass.

Holland cleared her throat as she waited for Anax Drew to look up.

"My dear?" he asked, surveying her from thick glasses, lingering too long on her lush hips.

I snarled, and Shae gripped my arm in warning. "Remember, Aether said this could be a test."

I forced a breath out through my lips. I didn't want this to be the Wish World. I wanted to live here, to be with Holland, always.

"I was instructed to find you. I've been appointed Dux by President Dale himself." Holland's melodic voice coated the room and my nerves alike.

"Did he?" Anax Drew leaned forward, sneering at her. "Well then, let's make it official."

He approached her from around the desk, and as he passed, his arm snaked out and gripped her ass. She yelped.

I snapped as I stormed closer, reaching for the anax only to find the floor expanding in real time, separating Holland and the slimy anax from my grasp.

"Holland!" I shouted as I attempted to move, to walk, to reach her, only to find it futile.

She was forever out of reach.

"I think you owe me a favor first, yes?" The anax propped himself up on the desk and began to unzip his pants.

"FUCK YOU!" I shouted at him. "GET AWAY FROM HER!"

Holland looked at me then and smiled. "Hi, Chance."

I froze. She saw me?

"Ho-Holland?" I stuttered her name as raw emotion choked my throat.

"Babe." She winked at me. "Don't worry about this asshole. I used compulsion to encourage him to say that to President Dale, and he got his punishment."

I blinked.

"So, this really happened?" I asked, viewing the room and scene in front of me in a new light.

"No. Yes. It's a variation of the past, your reimagination, and what you know of me, altered by this realm. But Chance." She took a step toward me, and the space submitted to her, allowing the distance to close. "It's dangerous here. You have to find the door. You must leave, now."

"What? No. I can't. *I won't* leave you, Holland. You were the only good thing in my life—my tether. I refuse to part with you ever again. I'd rather die here with you." I took a step and moved closer; the ground allowed it, and the space diminished until I was within reach of her.

"Chance," she said sadly as she extended her hand and braced it on my chest. I shuddered at her material touch. "You have to go. For me. You must."

Memories assaulted me. Things I wished to forget but couldn't.

"Take him, Shae," Holland spoke and then flexed her fingers on my chest. "Go now, Chance. Know I'll find you again, one way or another. What's lost is not gone."

I looked at her, but she pulsed and shoved me. I fell backwards and landed hard on my ass. I jumped to my feet, but the ground began rapidly growing, stretching out infinitely, and this time, Holland vanished from view. The office around us disappeared, giving way to dirt-covered ground, pine trees, and various structures.

I stood in the guaramen's yard.

"Chance, we have to find the door." Shae stood beside me, looking around the empty, dirt-filled space.

"No. We find Holland." I began stalking across the dirt-packed ground when I heard it: unnatural howls, moans, and the gnashing of teeth.

Swarms of beasts streamed through the forest, screeching in the night.

"CHANCE!" Shae shouted as ice formed at her fingers. I called my lightning, but nothing came.

Fuck!

Holland's scream sounded from ahead, "SAVE ME!"

I bolted toward the sound, ignoring Shae's warnings.

Various seethings pounced in front of me, but I paid them no heed. Instead, I ran toward Holland's distressed cries, even as large talons swiped at me, and I barely dodged their attacks. A beast landed in front of me, blocking my path, and lunging at me with its talons. I evaded its strike but fell prey to the next beast that sliced my side.

I winced as blood sprayed, coating the ground, and then a blast of ice sent the creature flying backwards.

"Chance. Where's the door?" Shae demanded as she sent spears of ice at the creatures, impaling their hearts.

A melody began playing above. A hard rock Winter Solstice song I grew up listening to, only this was accompanied by the steady tick of a giant clock.

I looked to the sky and noted a countdown, just over two minutes.

"We have to find it!" Shae shouted as she blasted another beast, and then another. I felt a tug to the left, as if that was where I needed to go.

"HELP!" Holland screamed. I bolted to the right, aiming toward her cries even if it was in the opposite direction of the internal tug.

"Chance! That's not her!" Shae shouted, but I ignored her.

Only one person mattered, and it wasn't me or Shae.

Beasts landed all around me, but I ran toward one and then ducked, rolled, and dodged its swipes before I kicked its foot, eliciting a howl, and sent it careening into the dirt. I didn't hesitate or fight the next oncoming seething and instead continued running toward Holland's pleas. I ran and ran and ran as Shea pelted icicles at the creatures closing in around us.

A dark cavern appeared with a single form inside it.

"Help me, Chance! I'm helpless! Save me!" Holland cried.

Wrong.

Something reeked.

Shae's hand was at my back, gripping my shirt as she erected a wall of ice behind us, blocking the creatures and their relentless attacks.

"It's not her, Chance. Holland would never say that."

The figure waved inside, extending a hand to me—wrong.

"You're right. She's a badass. She doesn't need me. I'm the one who needs her," I croaked the words as ire flared in my gut.

She was so much better than me.

The figure in the cave snarled and its eyes lit in an angry red hue. It stalked forward, and its hand became a ghostly claw. It leaned into the light, revealing a disfigured face that dripped vileness as black pus leaked from its broken jaw.

"But you were sooo close," it cooed and then threw back its head before releasing a torrent of vomit. Shae threw up an ice shield, blocking it, but the bile ate through it, along with the ground, almost as if it were pure acid.

"Poison," Shae called as she reinforced the icy wall with layer after layer. Seethings pounded at the back dome.

The melody surrounding us hit a new note, and the clock began a thirty-second countdown.

Holland's warning played through my mind; we needed to find the door.

I searched for the internal pull once more and then grabbed Shae's hand. "This way!"

She nodded at me tightly as she willed a dome to form through the ice, a tunnel just for us.

We ran through the forest, back the way we came but further out, and the entire time, Shae created a continuous ice tunnel to shield us, forming it as we ran. Seethings attacked the tunnel from all angles, some even piercing the ice with their thick talons, but we ignored them as we ran.

An unholy screech sounded behind us, shaking the very ice and ground we pounded, and then the tunnel filled with a putrid smell. Rancid vomit began to flood the tunnel, eating through Shae's reinforced layers of ice, forming a barrier behind us.

Tick.

Tick!

TICK!

The clock above continued its dooming countdown as the song nearly hit its final note.

Ahead a door shimmered brightly.

Shae saw it and neither of us spoke as we approached it. A gonging sounded, the sixth of the twelve strikes, reverberating all around and blending with the heightened electric guitar's final notes.

GONG!

Five seconds.

GONG!

Three seconds.

The vomit hit our feet, and I slipped, but Shae gripped my arm and lunged toward the door with me towing behind.

The door's energy flared.

The final note sounded.

Zapping power engulfed us as we entered the portal and twisted, falling through space.

I was nothing.

I'd always been nothing without her.

And then, my face hit a grainy wood plank, and I blinked.

"We made it." Shea heaved and patted my back.

I lay unmoving on the ground, staring at the tree in the corner.

"Shae, you're alright!" Tate's voice sounded.

I didn't look up and instead closed my eyes, wishing once more that my *love* was with me, here in my arms.

Despair threatened to overrun me, stop my heart, and it probably would have had it not been for the rage boiling over in my gut.

CHAPTER 6
TATE

"**T**ATE!" Shae exclaimed as she rushed into my arms. "That was...intense."

My arms tightened around her, releasing the breath I hadn't realized I'd been holding. "It was. What, uh," I cleared my throat as I stared at Chance, who still lay unmoving on the floor. "What happened to you guys?"

She pushed back from my arms and gazed at my face with haunted grey-blue eyes. "We were transported back in time, but it wasn't our past, it was..."

"Holland's," Chance rasped as he pressed up from the floor and snarled at me. "I got to see her only to be torn away once more."

"I'm so sorry, Chance, I—"

He rushed me, but Aether's solid body slammed into him and sent them both tumbling to the floor in a brawl. They rolled across the thick rug, grunting and punching without any apparent method, before Shae threw ice chips at them, and they jolted apart.

"Boys," she admonished. "This place is a test, yes? Nothing here is real. Or at least, it's not as it seems. I think we need to figure out how to get home."

"I agree." I nodded, swallowing. I loved being with Shae, but this place reeked unnaturally even with the façade of its cozy, Winter Solstice vibes.

"They don't deserve to breathe!" Chance roared, nostrils flaring.

Instinct had me taking a step back. An instant mistake as Aether's eyes tracked my movement, and his eyes lit with fire as he turned on Chance, prepared to attack once more, to add another cut to Chance's swollen lip. Shae threw an ice lasso at both males in the room and secured them with a huff.

She quirked a brow at me, but I had nothing to add. Selfishly, I was so grateful to be with my best friend once again—even if she came with *him*. But I also knew this place wasn't as it seemed. Where before the floorboards evaporated and faded into nothingness, now they were solid once more. The tree in the corner had also changed. Instead of sporting blood ornaments and red lights over a blue spruce, it was half its size with flickering, ominous, red lights and ornaments of crowns, flames, and swords.

I bit my lip as I pivoted to face the fireplace.

Where the 'T' and 'C' were lit before, now the 'S' and the 'A' vibrated wildly, and the flames in the hearth flared, flashing a brief pink. The second hovering door dropped from its position midair and impacted the floor with a *thud!* It flashed, and waves of mist and smoke poured from its opening, coating the floor and obscuring the wood, rug, and our feet.

A melody echoed through the door, loud and oddly comforting. Aether's eyes misted over a moment before he swallowed in somber acceptance. The mist flowed as if there was a river winding around the room, before wrapping around Aether's feet. He looked at me, solemn foreboding in his eyes.

"I'll go." He nodded toward the door, following the mist's lead.

"I'm coming."

"Tate—"

"Aether, I brought us to this Wish World. I'm not leaving you now."

"It could be a trap," he protested as his hulking form blocked the shimmering door.

Unlike the first door that was lit with a radiating golden light, this second door held a neutral shade of white that swirled and blurred, almost like that of mist, but was composed of pure energy, tiny, powerful molecules. It didn't pull me as the first had, but if my bonded was going, then so was I.

"Everything here could be a trap. *And* this also could be a test." I took a pointed step toward him. His jaw flexed, but he nodded. I glanced back at Shae one more time; she smiled at me, even as tears misted her eyes and worry gnawed at her lip.

"It'll be alright." My assurance fell flat, but still I turned, gripped Aether's hand, and stepped through the door with him.

CHAPTER 7
AETHER

"**A**ETHER," Tate's voice fluttered around me, loose, unembodied, and ethereal.

I was everything and nothing at the same time. Moisture licked at my face, coiled around my spine, and then a familiar tingle coated my skin. With a brief *zap!* my feet touched a smooth, solid surface.

I shook my head violently, and the mist cleared from my vision, but still swallowed my feet. Tate's form straightened next to me as she too observed our surroundings. We stood on a large terrace that overlooked the sea. A terrace I was acutely and intimately familiar with.

My home.

Memories washed over me as I recalled the first time I brought Tate here and showed her this space; the way she looked out at the sea and watched my dragon form approach, delight and wonder in her eyes that soon transitioned to lust as I shifted into my nude humanoid form.

I shook my head, quickly scouring the area for any threats. If I had my magic, I'd be able to *sense* any foreign presences—I'd be able to end them where they stood, strike them down, and choke the life from them without so much as lifting a hand.

But this wasn't reality.

This was the Wish World, and I wielded no magic here.

My eyes landed on the broken door leading to my bedroom. It lay on the ground in shards, its frame splintered. I paced across the large terrace, ignoring the glorious sea at my back, and strode into what was once my bedroom. The dark sheets and four-poster bed had been massacred. Shredded bits of silk and fur dotted the ground. The couch cushions had been slashed, the mattress gutted, and even the fireplace had been rummaged through.

My home.

My old home.

"Aether, I'm so sorry." Tate's voice was but a whisper as her tender hand rubbed my back.

"Not your fault." I scanned the room for any signs of new threats. The lurking shadows mocked me as I squinted at them, suspicion my constant companion. The damage here appeared a few weeks old, but you could never be too certain. Whoever did this and broke through my runes, they were strong enough magically to enter and had enough power to ensure it was fully decimated.

My bet was on the vile female who coveted power and was a constant threat to the Embassy and my mate, Tate.

I grabbed Tate's hand in mine, and together we paced through the trashed room.

"This was your home, Aether. I feel responsible—"

"Tate," I said as I stopped and turned, cupping her face in both of my hands. "*You're* my home."

Tears swelled in her eyes, and I leaned in and took her lips in mine.

Gentle, firm, and passionate.

She softened into my touch, leaned into my warmth, and offered what comfort she could through her devotion.

Hesitantly, I pulled back. I didn't want to—not in the least. But we weren't safe here. This was the Wish World. What occurred was unknown and didn't follow nature's laws.

"I love you," she spoke before she sniffed and swatted at her eyes.

"I love you, too." I gripped her hand once more, and we continued through the destroyed home.

The living area was somehow worse. Every piece of furniture had been broken and destroyed. The couch, end tables, lamps, blankets, sconces, and even the stone wall had been violated.

The kitchen counter was split down the middle, but that wasn't them—*that* was me. Us. I smiled at Tate as the memory flashed before my eyes.

"That one at least was our doing." I winked at Tate as I gave her hand a squeeze. "I actually have several good memories here."

Tate snorted and shook her head sheepishly. "Like what?"

I went to send her a mental image down the bond and then cursed myself for forgetting we didn't have that ability here.

"Like when you stood right there and sheepishly wondered if I drank my own blood."

"Aether!" She smacked my shoulder playfully.

"I already adored you, but at that point, there was absolutely no return for me. You had me hook, line, and sinker."

She bumped me with her hips as she eyed the kitchen, likely replaying the same memory as I was.

"I can't wait to get out of the Wish World, Aether. I want to be able to show you what I'm thinking."

"Same."

I turned and led us through the rubble, stepping over shards of wood, glass, and stones until we reached the front door. There, pinned into the center of the fractured wood, was a flyer:

TRAITOR! AETHER BRYCHAN IS HEREBY SENTENCED TO DEATH FOR HIS BETRAYAL. ANYONE SEEN HARBORING HIM OR HIS COMPANIONS WILL MEET THE SAME FATE.

I swallowed as I tore the parchment from the nail on the door.

"Fuck, Aether, this is bad," Tate murmured.

"We knew she would pin things on us. Let's just get out of here."

Tate nodded, and I crumpled the parchment in my fist before chucking it into the rubble behind me.

We stepped out into the dark street, lit dimly by various light posts. Tate's hand grabbed mine as we slunk down the narrow road, pressing our backs close to the stone wall, until we reached a door that led to James and Uley's house—Ruby's home.

Swallowing, I stared at the splintered door. A similar note was pinned to its center:

TRAITORS TO THE EMBASSY. IF SPOTTED, NOTIFY THE CHAIRS IMMEDIATELY.

"Fuck, Aether, this is *really* bad. But they're safe. If they're still searching for them, then they're safe."

I forced a tight breath through my lips and nodded once in agreement. I poked my head through the doorway—the entire home appeared to be in similar shape as mine, destroyed.

Squaring tense shoulders, I turned and led Tate through the street. This was the Wish World, I reminded myself. Not reality. Though this certainly felt closer to what I feared was occurring back at the Embassy at the present moment. We continued to move through the abandoned city. Not a single soul sounded, no laughter, no voices, nothing.

This had to be a test.

Everything thus far has been a test, this included. A test for *me* this time. I reached reflexively for my sword only to find none. That wouldn't do. We made a left down a small alley, and I located one of the changing sheds strategically placed near a training ground for dragon shifters. The door creaked open loudly, far too loud for the still night. I rummaged through it as Tate stared intently at the shadows, daring them to try something. Clothes, tunics, pants, belts, and...a condom? I rolled my eyes and almost gave up when my hand hit something hard wrapped in leather. I pulled the long object out and practically shouted as I beheld a sword with a small dagger strapped to the long sheath.

"Gold." I pulled out the dagger and handed it to Tate, who merely quirked a brow. I unsheathed the sword, savoring its weight in my hand.

I was no longer helpless.

"Really? I get the dagger?" She flipped it with grace, showcasing her improved skill with blades. "I think I can handle a sword, *Aether*."

"I'm sure. But there's only one, so let's let the sword master have it, yes?"

"Agreed. So, hand it over then." She extended her hand.

I scoffed, and she chuckled before tossing the dagger at my form. I didn't move, trusting her aim, as she pinned the blade to the door directly behind my head and just to the side. A smile tugged at my lips as she smirked, sauntering the few feet over to me before leaning in close as she reached behind me to get the blade that nearly grazed my ear.

"I'll let you keep the sword." She exhaled slowly as she yanked the dagger free. With it secure in her palm, she lifted up on her toes and pecked my cheek before taking a step back and examining the mist once more.

Slowly, I released a deep, contented breath and then adjusted my grip on the sword.

"Let's get out of here." My voice came out rougher than intended.

This place was messing with me.

We crept through another eerily quiet alley and rounded a corner when a wave of fog hit us square in the face. With it came an acidic scent and voices.

Whispers.

All around us, hushed voices spoke in languages I couldn't understand.

"Aether..." Tate spoke, back going rigid and dagger at the ready as she surveyed the living mist.

A wisp of mist reached out and wrapped around her wrist. She swatted at it with her hand, but it constricted. She sliced it free from her with the dagger.

The enveloping voices became louder, and the language intelligible.

"TRAITORS!"

I sliced a tendril reaching out for me with my blade and then gripped Tate's elbow and began running through the mist.

"VILE!"

"EVIL!"

"FAILURES!"

The voices rose from whispers to screams, engulfing us whole as wisps of mist solidified and then coiled throughout the vapor, reaching for us, willing our feet to be rendered immobile. I sliced at the living vines with my sword, and they hissed in response. Tate stabbed at the corporeal whips of white energy with her dagger, and they hissed as her aim struck true.

"Which way, Aether?" Tate shouted, cutting a tether that managed to grab her left arm with her dagger and then stabbing another rising vine.

Which way? I silenced the rising panic clawing at my throat and instead focused on the internal pull.

Right.

We needed to go right.

A tendril of mist, the width of my arm, rose from the ground and began dancing as it darted toward Tate. I lifted my sword and cut it at its root, and then diced it as it lay on the wet ground.

"This way!" I shouted and nodded right to the alley. Tate nodded once, stabbed another vine of energy, and then darted in the direction I indicated, with me by her side.

I followed the pull, leading us through the city, even as the voices rose behind us in a haunting wave of pain, hatred, and ire.

A shimmer occurred ahead, and this time, instead of a rope or vine of mist, an entire figure emerged from the materialized mist, formed of solidified water vapor—milky white with haunting, black eyes.

It continued to grow and shrink until it wasn't just a random humanoid figure, but one I intimately recognized.

"Son," the voice hissed, sounding like broken wind. "You failed again. You've betrayed your country. You're such a pathetic excuse of life."

I snarled as I lifted the sword, prepared to end him for the second time.

He merely laughed as he paced closer; the shrill voices from behind blurred into unknown languages once more, surrounding us and tickling our skin with their acidic tongues.

"You can't kill me here, boy. But I can hurt you. I can hurt *her*." He pointed a hand toward Tate, and a tendril grew from it, spearing straight for her.

"FUCK YOU!" I shouted as I sliced at the vine and then the next, and the next, and the next.

"You really are such a disappointment." My father tsked. "I would've thought you'd be able to see this for what it was. A distraction."

I pivoted, and Tate was gone.

"TATE!" I screamed her name as I searched every angle, every direction, for my bonded.

Only white met my eyes. That and the haunting vision of teary eyes from the wailing forms of the impalpable creatures gathering around me.

"Where is she?" I charged the misty father figure and stabbed his gut. A pleasing resistance met my blade, but then he evaporated and reformed behind me, laughing. Mocking.

"TATE!" I screamed. "*What did you do?!*" I demanded.

Panic seared my insides, stabbed my heart, and nearly stalled my breath. This couldn't be happening.

"You're not good enough for her. Why should you, a *mut*, end up with her? If she's to rule, she'll need someone *else* by her side. Someone better." He sneered and then released two snake-like creatures from his hands. They slithered across the ground on their path toward me.

I reached for my magic and found none. What was worse was the reminder that I couldn't feel the bond; I couldn't feel Tate.

I slashed the two serpents with skilled strikes and then pivoted and beheaded the figure that looked and sounded like my father.

His head dropped to the ground at the same time Tate's scream met my ears.

"TATE!" I roared.

I paused, forced myself to remain unmoving for a moment. This was the Wish World. This was a test. I needed to find her, and that meant following the pull.

A loud song began blaring all around, drowning out the sound of the crying voices wailing everywhere and simultaneously nowhere. White oozed from my father's body's stump, bleeding across the stone ground, burning and singeing before it ate the very stones. Everywhere it touched, a black bottomless hole appeared.

The melody, a traditional Winter Solstice carol that my mother would sing to me as a child, began to play. Its notes grew louder, wrapping around my body and willing my feet forward.

I turned around and began to run straight through the mist and fog, only seeing a few feet ahead of me. A loud ticking sounded above.

The clock.

Tate would be fine.

"I'm coming!" I shouted as I followed the pull. I made a left, then a right, then another right. My feet hit small black pebbles as I entered a new area. Black stone walls stood erect in front of me. The mist thinned enough to see twenty feet ahead this time, allowing me to see that I was on the outskirts of a maze.

I was in the arena.

"TATE!" I shouted as the clock hit a loud *TICK!*

My mother's voice drifted around me, singing the tune she'd sing the night before the solstice.

"Just another woman you failed. You're pathetic." My father's voice drifted around, impalpable.

My left hand shook with barely restrained rage.

My mother's voice continued to sing.

The clock ticked.

"TATE!" I screamed her name as I began maneuvering through the maze, sword at the ready.

"AETHER!" Her scream met my ears, and a new urgency moved my feet, so I was running through the maze, following only an inexplicable compass's guide.

A figure draped in black appeared ahead, blocking my path. Unlike the other abstract beings, this one was tangible, material. Her hair was braided and coiled around her head, blonde at the roots and black at the tips.

She smirked at me.

"Juda?" I moved closer, sword lowered but still threatening.

"Chair, now," she spat at me and then willed flames to form at her fingertips. "I'm the Chair now. Who knew?" She took a step closer to me, flames building from her fingers.

Tate screamed, and my heart hammered.

"Move," I commanded.

A wave of liquid, black flames flew at me, and I barely ducked and rolled in time.

"Juda! Let me pass."

"Fuck you, Aether. Everyone always said you'd be the next Chair; they wrote me off. Well, you know what? No more."

Another volley of flames poured from her hands. I lunged away, but the heat licked at my back and ate my clothing, searing as it did so, no doubt burning.

Fuck it.

Before she readied her next wave, I picked up a large stone and charged her. I threw it, and she easily evaded, but the distraction was all I needed to close the distance. Within two heartbeats, my sword was protruding through her middle. She gasped as blood began to spurt from her lips, coating her front.

"You'll never save her." She coughed and then went limp.

I tore my blade from her stomach and let her body crumble to the pebbled ground. The clock's ticking grew louder, and the melody still wrapping around me hit its final chorus.

Time was running out.

I ran. With all my might, all my skill, and every ounce of energy, I pushed forward on the loose pebbles, plowing through the maze like a projectile.

Shadow Tribe figures emerged in my path, but I cut them down. One after another. I silenced any guilt as I reminded myself this wasn't real, they weren't real, but a figment, a test of this damned place.

I made a final left and then entered the center of the maze. There, strapped to a metal chair in the middle, was Tate.

My father gripped her chin in his hands, and I stared once more at the monster who would forever haunt me.

A monster I'd already slain.

Tate attempted to bite his fingers, and he simply pulled his hand back and laughed before backhanding her.

I charged.

My father leered at me as he threw out his hands, and waves of black flames barreled straight for me.

I rolled and then stood, but the flames followed. They licked at my skin, and I couldn't stop the sounds of agony slipping from my lips.

Tate shouted for me, and my father simply laughed more.

"He looks like me, dear, but I assure you, he's only half the male. A mistake."

The air around me gripped my feet and tore the blade from my hands.

My mother's honey voice began singing the song's outro as the clock sounded its first *gong!*.

If I had my power, my father would be dead already.

The energy wrapping around my legs lifted me higher in the air and held me suspended upside down. My father approached from below, sneering up at me.

"Aether, this was too fucking easy. You failed, my boy."

A door appeared behind Tate and flashed as the third gong sounded. Tate nodded to me as she flicked her wrist and cut through the binding at her hands with her dagger, my father ignorant of her progress.

This was a test, I reminded myself.

This was the Wish World.

What was I missing? I searched within myself and realization dawned.

"You're right. I'm not enough. I'm imperfect and she deserves more." At my words, my father's eyes flared and the grip he held on me faltered. Just enough for me to pull free and tumble to the ground. Black flames engulfed me as the gong sounded its sixth time, and the door shuddered.

I gripped the hilt of my sword, ignoring the pain from the fire, and chucked it to Tate.

The flames vanished, and my father stalked toward my shaking, burnt form.

"Time for vengeance, yes?" He extended one hand and cut off the air from my throat as his other hand readied a ball of condensed fire.

The clock hit its ninth chime, and then metal sliced through my father's neck. The sword lodged halfway, but it was enough. He fell to the ground, his hold on me gone, as he pawed at the sword stuck in his neck before falling forward.

"AETHER!" Tate rushed me, but I held up my hand.

"The door." I stood, noting the frame's flickering and the light beginning to fade.

I gripped Tate's hand and ran, ignoring the pain of my skin tearing with each movement, and instead allowed the adrenaline to carry me forward. Tate's steps were sure, and she reached the portal at the start of the twelfth *gong!*

My mother's melodic voice hit her final note.

Tate's body entered the portal, and she vanished, pulling my hand through the door with her. My chest hit the portal and became lodged, stuck against a thick, resistant wall of energy; only my hand had vanished.

I was too late.

The door flickered, but my hand remained hidden. I felt a tug, and then my whole body went flying into the portal.

Pain tore at my being, eating me, rearranging me, redefining me. I screamed, but no sound came, nothing but darkness and pain. And then a force threw me forward, and I saw a light. A small door with a long rope reached out to me. Only, it wasn't a rope. It was an arm, mine and Tate's, our joined hands the tether.

My anchor in everything.

My bonded.

She tugged, and my body began flying toward the door that grew larger and larger until our arms weren't impossibly long but normal length, and I fell into the embrace of my mate.

She stumbled backwards, and we landed on a thick rug in the cabin.

My heart pounded, and I pushed against the ground and searched her for any harm.

Warm mahogany eyes looked at me with reverence.

"Why?" Moisture began building in my eyes as I stared at my perfect bonded. "I'm unworthy."

"Aether." She cupped my face in her hands and willed me closer. "You're perfect. You're everything I could ever hope for. And you're more than enough."

Her lips were tender as she kissed me. I leaned into the kiss, into her warmth. Her body responded to mine and began to rock beneath me.

With one hand, I cradled her head and deepened the kiss, savoring every ounce of her. The other hand dug into the rug, keeping the brunt of my weight from her.

She wrapped her legs around me and began to moan in my mouth.

That was it. My undoing.

I moved to my knees and tore my shirt off, then pants. Tate did the same and then stood on uneven feet, gloriously nude in the cabin lit only by the flames in the fire and the flickering, twinkling lights on the tree behind her.

Her breasts were perky, round, and heavy—begging me to savor them and show her the worship she was due.

My cock hardened further to the point of pain, and I moved closer to my prey.

She smirked at me and then turned, flaunting her perfectly plump ass and curves, before looking over her shoulder. "Well? What are you waiting for?"

I rushed her, and she giggled as my hands wrapped around her waist. I picked her up, swung her around in the air, and then lowered her body to the lush rug directly in front of the fire.

"Any preference?" I asked, voice heated.

"Just fucking take me." Her voice broke at the end as she moaned when my cock pressed against her entrance but didn't enter. "Aether—"

I leaned down and took the bud of her breast into my mouth and sucked as I continued to grind my body across hers with the most delightful friction. I may not have the ability to manipulate energy here, but I could bring her pleasure with my bare body. I was a proud male after all, well-hung at that.

I reached down to her thigh and lifted it as my stomach brushed her clit. She gasped in delight, and I repeated the motion, pulling her breast deeper into my mouth and then gently nipping at it before licking it better.

"Oh, Mother Blood, Aether—"

"That's fucking right. Say my name."

I reveled in the way her eyes rolled back in pleasure. The way her lips parted in a moan, and her body quivered.

I released her from my mouth and then pulled her hips closer to my body. With a teasing finger, I tested her core—deliciously wet.

I smirked at her as I toyed with her, pumping with my fingers as she writhed before me—lit beautifully in orange firelight.

"Please...come..."

"Hmmm," I growled as I expertly stroked her insides and flicked her clit at the same time before releasing her and toying with the tender spots on her thighs.

"Fuck—Aether—You bastard!"

I laughed and then gave her what she craved. I thrusted, allowing my cock to fill her fully. At the first thrust, her hands braced the rug.

"YES!" Her voice floated throughout the rustic cabin.

"Like that?" I asked as I pounded again and again.

"Ye-Yes!"

I thrusted once more before dropping down, so my face was just above hers. "And this?"

"Oh blood---yes!"

My male ego flared, and I lifted her body into my arms before pivoting so I was below her and she was above, riding me. She threw her head back, allowing her pink-tipped, golden hair to cascade down her back. Wisps fell in front and blocked part of her bouncing breasts as she rode me. I thrusted with each of her passes, her fingers digging into my chest.

She tensed and then shuddered as she came. The sensation was too much. Pleasure erupted, and I grunted as I too orgasmed with my bonded, my one and only, my forever.

She rode her waves of pleasure, and my euphoric state heightened as I watched the ecstasy cross her features. Slowly, she stopped moving and then looked down at me; her eyes twinkled in the firelight.

She was truly a goddess.

I lifted a hand and cupped her cheek.

She nuzzled into it before lowering herself to my chest, where I wrapped both my arms around her body and held her tight, secure.

The fire roared and we lay there in silence for just a moment, embracing one another in the only good moment we'd had in the Wish World yet.

As if the thought summoned them and cursed our existence, the door flared with life.

"Fuck!" I moved to cover Tate's body as two figures were flung through the door.

CHAPTER 8

CHANCE

"CHANCE, where are we?" Shae asked, standing in easily the grandest hallway I'd ever seen.

A polished floor that screamed OCD expanded in front of us in a seemingly unending hallway. Large ornate portraits graced each side of the hallway, each one housing a different ethereal figure—most of which were adorned with crowns.

"I don't know. But I don't like it," I grumbled. Stepping through the door had been a mistake. Ending up in the Wish World had been a mistake, something I'd kill Tate for had it not been for those few moments where I was with Holland.

The stupid part of my heart thought I'd get to see her again by stepping through the portal. I was wrong. Wherever we were, I'd never been here before—I doubted we were even in Shappa anymore.

"These look like royal portraits, Chance. And this looks like a palace. Which palace did you take us to?" Shae examined various depictions of richly robed people, all clothed in various shades of pink. Several boasted golden crowns upon their heads, and some even showed the rulers upon their thrones with descriptions like 'Just' or 'Fair' on rose gold plaques beneath each portrait.

"I don't know. If I had it my way, we'd be back with Holland. Not here." I spat a wad of saliva on the immaculate floor and then continued pacing down the eerie hallway. It was quiet, unnervingly so. "Just be ready for the other shoe to drop."

"Right." Shae increased her pace and then paused in front of a portrait in the hallway. A woman stood staring longingly at nothing. Her eyes held a deep red note but were somehow burnt. In the background, various white buildings were depicted and the sun was uniquely *pink*. Shappa. This depiction had to be of the Embassy. My eyes darted to the nameplate below it.

LADY ESME, ROYAL MEMBER AND OVERSEER OF THE EMBASSY.

"Chance, she looks like Tate." Shae arched a brow at me as she reached out to caress the painted face. "Like, an uncanny resemblance to Tate. You don't think..."

"Fuck. I know where we are," I growled as I tore the painting from the wall and sent it scattering across the floor. "This is that bitch's homeland. Mydant."

"What? How?" Shae knelt to pick the portrait up, but I grabbed her arm and yanked her upright.

"I don't know, but it doesn't matter. Let's just find the door and get out of this blood-forsaken place."

I stormed ahead of her, feet clicking against the annoyingly pristine tile, and then finally reached a large double door. The moment my feet breached the frame's barrier, the world flickered, and I found myself standing on a sand pit with colosseum seating surrounding it. A platform stood proudly in the corner with four chairs placed on it.

"I wasn't expecting this..." Shae's voice echoed in the empty arena.

"Yeah, well, let's keep moving—"

A screech sounded from above. My eyes searched the sky until I spotted a large creature circling. It lowered as it moved, roaring once more and lighting up the sky with unique pink flames. I pivoted to retreat, but the door we'd entered through was nowhere to be seen. More flames ate up the sky and reached for the sand near us, nearly scorching our forms. I scanned the arena and then spotted a door across the way.

"Shae! This way!" I shouted as I began to sprint across the sand pit. The large entrance lay directly ahead. We needed to reach it before—

Fire blasted in front of me, stopping my tracks and sending Shae careening into me. We rolled together across the sand, and the air left my lungs.

I lay there, momentarily stunned.

Shocked.

Shook.

The ground shuddered, and the beast touched down, blocking our path to the door. It lowered its neck toward Shae and me, then shook its head back and forth in a serpent's motion.

"We need to go back!" Shae shot to her feet.

I couldn't bring myself to move. Part of me wanted to surrender, to allow the dragon to burn me alive and end it all. It'd be a fitting end to this hellish life.

The beast locked eyes with mine, its pink-ringed irises triggering my memories. The only other time I'd seen pink haloed eyes was when my father died. When *she* died.

"FUCK YOU!" I screamed at the dragon as I found my feet and took a challenging step closer. "TATE! You better kill me before I fucking kill you!"

The dragon huffed, mocking me.

"Chance, what the hell are you thinking? We need to go. Now!" Shae gripped my arm and attempted to tug me back.

"No. Even if I wanted to leave, Shae, the pulling I feel leads past the dragon. There's no way but through *her*." I ripped my arm from Shae's grasp and moved closer to the dragon, who snarled.

I'd always feared Tate was stronger than I realized. That her power was unrivaled. That she could shift like *they* could, the Untish.

"You will not survive. You are nothing. You've always been nothing." An unknown voice wafted around us, sounding from everywhere and nowhere at once.

"I'M THE PRESIDENT!" I screamed, my voice ricocheting from the stands.

Above, new figures appeared, dragons getting closer. Various colored flames lit up the sky, and their roars reverberated throughout the colosseum —shaking the sand my feet were loosely planted on.

Only the president because you failed. Failed your father. Failed your love. You're the monster, Chance. You've always been a vile thing, and just wait until you look like one of them.

My body shook and the dragon opened its jaw, flames lighting its throat. Pain snapped from within, racing through my veins, lighting me on fire from the inside. I dropped to my knees, Shae's screams along with the ice coating the sand became background, and the dragon released her flames. They flew at me, the heat searing and endless. I closed my eyes and surrendered, prepared for my end. The voices had been right. I was nothing. I was—

The flames passed my body, and the stabbing pain ceased. I opened my eyes to see a black, scaled wing in front of me, blocking the flames and the dragon. What the—

I looked at my hands and noted long talons protruding from where each finger should be.

I was a monster.

"Oh, dear blood," Shae's voice whispered from behind. An icy shield covered her, and the one she'd built in front of me had completely melted, succumbed to the flames.

I pivoted, savoring the ease with which my body moved, the way I could turn and glide with minimal effort. Amazing.

"Chance, what happened?" Shae's fingers frosted over, and ice began to surround us, blocking the dragon even though its flames could eat through the ice with minimal contact.

"Don't you know? I'm a monster." I laughed bitterly, feeling the strange feeling of four fangs protruding from my mouth.

A song started to weave above. One I'd listened to during the Winter Solstice back when I first joined the guara. It was a rock and roll beat that somehow felt festive.

Well, holly fucking yay.

Time to dance.

I turned to face off with the dragon, whose eyes merely squinted as she prepared another wave of flames. The ground beneath me shook, sending Shae falling into my winged, scaled back, as another dragon lowered. One covered in black scales. I glared at the beast, cursed his scar and the male I knew it represented, before focusing on Tate once more.

Shae pushed off my scaled body, leaving the distinct feeling of ice coating my back. It was almost refreshing in this form. *Almost.*

"Ready to see what you've done, Tate? You've created monsters. You've spread evil, and now it runs wild while you hide out in your castle." I laughed bitterly. "I think not." As I spoke the final words, I charged her. My feet ate at the sand.

Shae screamed from behind me as new flames erupted from Tate. Shae sent a wall of ice in front of me, the flames destroying it in an instant, but my wings blocked the fire as I rolled. Shae fled to the perimeter, where she was safe in a dome of ice that moved with her. I extended my talons and charged the pink dragon, prepared to tear into her hide, when a blur hit me from the side and sent me flying two hundred feet into the stands. My body impacted the wooden seats, splintering them, as I burrowed deeper into the benches until my momentum halted. I shook my head in time to see black flames flying toward me.

"NO!" I seethed as I flung myself upwards and, to my delight, my wings carried me.

I could fucking fly.

Shae attempted to stop the black dragon with lassoes made of ice, but it was pointless—the dragon simply burned them away.

"Go!" I shouted at her. She hesitated a moment, looking between me and the door behind the pink dragon.

The black dragon thrashed its head and then bellowed liquid flames at me. I evaded them, climbing higher, and the black dragon launched into the air, hot on my heels. I pumped my wings harder, faster, and climbed into the clouds—noting various dragons circling all around. They began to close in on me, talons opened, readied.

That's when I fell. I tucked in my wings and spiraled down, barely evading their opened claws, the same ones that would shred my entrails if given the chance, as I plummeted downwards like a heavy projectile aimed for the sandy arena. The black dragon followed me closely as I approached the pink dragon in the stadium far below.

Shae moved toward the door in the back, ice forming a protective wall between her and the dragon.

The wind blew past my face, tore at my scaled wings, and sent ecstasy soaring through my blood. What a fucking shame, the only way I could experience this was because *she* made me a monster.

The colosseum came closer, and I flared my wings, nearly impacting the seating, before finding my balance and soaring past Tate, dragging my claws across her back and delighting in her roar, before scooping up Shae in my arms and soaring through the door.

Flames ate at my back, would have killed me had it not been for my wings and Shae's protective ice barrier.

We crossed the threshold, and my wings vanished; my bloodied talons disappeared, and we impacted a wooden floor, skittering across its splintered, dusty surface. New pain laced my body, and I pressed up from the floor, noting new scrapes and blood leaking from my fleshy arms—gone was my monster form. Liquid dripped down my chin, and I swiped at it, clearing the scruff from its fresh iron coat.

"What the fuck was that!" Shae shouted at me as she stood, brushing off the sand and blood coating her pants and shirt.

"Metamorphosis," I responded dryly.

"Chance, you tried to kill her! What's wrong with you?"

"I'm who she made me, Shae."

I tuned out her response as I surveyed the room. It was quaint, small, and homey. A small bed sat in the corner with a quilted cover. A desk stood next to it, tidy with nothing but a notebook and pen beside it. An apron hung over a hook next to the desk, and a small wooden door was ajar. A voice echoed from inside. Sweet, harmonious, and somehow blended with the escalating rock and roll beat still thrumming loudly—even louder than before. In fact, the annoying tick-tock of the clock sounded too. Time was close to being up.

Curiosity and an inexplicable tug drew me to the small door. I peered inside. A short female with golden-brown eyes stood in front of a mirror, combing her light brown hair as she sang. Her frame was small, squared almost, but dainty. Like...Holland.

"Chance, the door!" Shae's voice called from behind as the energy in the room rippled.

The melody beating loudly above hit its final notes, and the clock began to *gong!*

But my eyes couldn't leave the sweet female singing her melody, carefree and content. Her almond eyes snapped up to mine in the mirror. She smiled, dimples forming at each side of her face.

"Holland?" I whispered. Knowing it wasn't her, but the resemblance was uncanny.

"No." She laughed softly. "Come find me, Chance."

Before I could respond, arms wrapped around my waist and yanked me backwards. I was falling, and panic clawed through my heart. I needed to know *who* she was.

Before I could find my footing, energy zapped my skin, and we were floating in a portal. Blackness swallowed all, engulfed me, and reformed around me. Everything became unknown.

A bright light appeared ahead, and then I was sucked into it and spat out onto a furry rug in a cabin I hated.

"FUCK!" a voice I loathed shouted.

I jumped to my knees and lunged for the door, only for the portal to close, becoming empty of magic, allowing me to fall through its hollow frame, where I landed on the cabin's wooden floor.

"Uh, guys. Better, you know, cover up," Shae spoke from behind.

I pivoted, eyes searching the empty frame for any sign of a way back to that female with her haunting eyes and honeyed voice.

But it was useless. This world was as cruel as the real one. She was gone.

CHAPTER 9
TATE

"TATE, that looked like *fun*," Shae teased as she bumped my now clothed body.

I rolled my eyes even though I didn't mind her teasing. It was one of her traits that I loved the most. If only I could bring her back with me to Mydant, secure her away where she was safe. Away from that raving lunatic currently sulking in the corner with his arms crossed and immaterial steam radiating from his tense form.

"Yeah, well, what can I say. How about you? How are you and Nora?" I asked, turning the conversation serious.

"Fine." Her eyes evaded my gaze, and she began to fidget with her fingernails, frost collecting across her skin.

"What does she think of the..." I cleared my throat. "Ice."

"She's 'cool'." Shae wagged her brows, but the effort did little to relieve the stress holding her shoulders captive.

"Mhmm. Well, I'm glad you're both good. We're going to find a way, you know. I'm going to get back to you or bring you back or—"

"NOT IF I DON'T FUCKING KILL YOU FIRST!" Chance raged from the couch where ropes of ice wrapped around his mid-section, legs, and arms, securing him.

"Don't you DARE speak to her like that," Aether snarled, attempting to stalk across the small cabin toward Chance, but ice secured his feet in place.

Shae's forehead glistened with a sheen of ice, and her usual grey-blue eyes were haloed in a frosted, icy blue as she focused on wielding her magic.

"Why do you think you're the only one who can wield?" I asked, glancing once more at the living vines of ice that did Shae's bidding.

"I don't know. Out of all of us, I'm the one who *doesn't* want the power." She blew a stray lock of hair from her eyes. "But fate is funny like that."

I nodded to her sentiment.

The tree in the corner flickered, and then the lights flared before completely dying, leaving the branches dark and the ornaments obscured in shadows.

The third door dropped from midair and impacted the floor. It hummed but didn't light up.

I swallowed as my eyes met Aether's dark, haunted ones. What we'd seen in the last door was...hard. On both of us, but to witness his bare, raw fears and insecurities lived out in front of him? It nearly destroyed me.

If this third door was as cruel, I wanted nothing to do with it. And yet, if I were to guess by the shaking floorboards and the flickering, roaring fire, we wouldn't have much of a choice.

"Shae, what happened to you guys?" I whispered, leaning into my friend, my sister in many ways.

"Shit." She huffed. "I mean, we ended up in some castle and saw a couple of dragons and Chance like freaked out—"

"We went to Mydant." Chance glared at me. "And you tried to kill me because you couldn't handle what *you* created."

"FUCK YOU!" Aether shouted, his restraints straining as he leaned forward. If he had his magic, Chance would already be dead. But then again, Chance would have his lightning, and this whole cabin would be basking in flames.

"Boys!" Shae shouted, erecting a wall of solid ice between them. "Enough."

The ice from the wall flowed, coated the floor, the rug, and nipped at my booted feet. I stepped closer to the fire that seemed to keep the cold at bay.

"So, Nora's good?" I clarified, noting the worry creasing Shae's face as she struggled to control the ice covering her arms and cheeks as her eyes turned a living shade of periwinkle blue.

"I don't know. I can't...control it, not all the way." Her jaw clenched. "But she insisted on sticking by my side, and I can't for the life of me understand what I did to deserve her loyalty through all of this." She gestured to the ice now creeping up the tree, Aether's legs, Chance's arms, and covering the couch.

"You'll figure this out. If anyone can, it's you, Shae." I stepped closer to her, but she jumped back and held her hands up.

"Don't!" She swallowed as her hands shook. "I don't want to hurt you."

"Shae." I grabbed her arm tenderly and smiled, refusing to flinch at the unnatural chill. "I'm not afraid. You shouldn't be either. If I could learn to control my magic and wield flames, then you can too."

A half smile tugged at her now blue lips.

"Seriously, I think—"

The floor shuddered, the door pulsed, and then a dark energy began pouring from the door, swallowing the ground and pulling the ice *into* its dark void.

Shae yelped as the inky waves of energy wrapped around her and then, with a solid tug, pulled her into the void.

"SHAE!" I screamed her name as I rushed after her.

"Tate, no!" Aether shouted, but his voice vanished behind me as the ominous cloud of energy wrapped around my feet and yanked me into the portal right after Shae.

I glanced back and briefly saw Aether's face, devastated, along with Chance's manic gaze. Then nothing but black waves of energy became everything as my very being was condensed, stretched, and then reformed. I heaved a heavy breath as I felt the energy shoving me forward toward a light.

A moment later, I stood on rubble, Shae at my side.

The entire Glenn was before us, completely wasted.

CHAPTER 10

TATE

"**T**ATE, I'm so sorry. I didn't mean for you to—"

"Shae." I held up my hand, stepping cautiously over several scattered rocks and various rubble. "This isn't your fault. I'm the one who brought us to this Wish World."

She locked her jaw as she surveyed the ruins. The entire city had been leveled. Not a single skyscraper had survived the decimation. The entire place was covered in glass, rubble, barbed spikes, and...bones. Bones littered the ground.

I looked closer to what I was standing on and gagged. Bile rose in my throat as I jumped backwards, away from the half-decayed arm I'd been standing on.

"Shae, what's happened? Is this what the Glenn actually looks like?"

Horror claimed me, skittered across my mind, and tightened my throat.

"No. It's bad, but not *this* bad. There's still half the city, this is...the Glenn's gone." Shae moved carefully, avoiding the corpses and partially decayed limbs dotting the heap of rubble we stood on.

I followed her, noting the smoke-filled air and the dots flying high in the sky above, circling the still-smoking debris. We made our way down the mound and into the sprawling ruins. Remnants of partial walls stood here and there, but everything had been torched. Shredded clothing, iron-stained ground and boulders, and broken signs marred the ground.

I forced the anger rising in my gut back down. *She* may not be accessible here, my beast form, but I could still feel a flash of her anger—her desire to shift and kill those responsible for this atrocity.

You're partially responsible...

I ignored my internal voice as a piece of paper hit my boots. I picked it up and froze. It was announcing a mandatory enlistment for *every* able-bodied vampire in the Glenn. No exceptions. If you chose not to enlist, you'd join the army of seethings.

"Shae, is the Glenn fully at war?" I gestured from the paper to the destroyed city.

She took the piece of soiled paper, and her brows arched together.

"I don't know, Tate. I mean, Chance was building an army, and I knew things were trending bad, but...wait, look!" She pointed to a date on the corner.

"That can't be right." I blinked as I stared at the date.

"Tate, this poster is from two years in the *future*."

"So, this is what the future looks like?" I refused to believe that. "No. I won't allow it."

Shae crumpled the paper and chucked it to the side before moving once more through the ruined city streets. I followed her, swallowing back the guilt, demanding I heave any of my stomach contents all over the already charred ground.

A figure landed ahead, atop a hill in the near distance, but even from here, I knew his frame.

His golden hair was cropped short, and he wore a presidential cape. He laughed, and the sound echoed throughout the rubble.

Chance.

"Stay close," Shae warned, an icicle forming in her left hand.

"Right." I pulled my shirt up to minimize the reek emanating from this blood-ruined place.

As a vampire, the scent of iron was usually intoxicating. But in this setting? With littered bodies dotting the ground? It was nauseating.

Chance raised his hands and screamed, calling forth red lightning bolts from the sky, sending them pounding into the already soured ground. One red bolt after another hit, and then ten struck at once. Everything went blindingly red.

I shielded my eyes with my hand as Shae gasped. His bolts hit the remaining trees dotting the hill, and they went up in flames—destroyed.

"Chance, nooo," Shae said sadly. She began moving faster toward him, and trepidation clawed at my heart.

It wasn't safe. Not without magic. But...Shae had magic.

"Stay here, Tate," Shae called over her shoulder.

"No way. You're not getting rid of me that fast."

"Tate—"

"No. I'm with you to the end, Shae." I spoke with reverence, and from the softening in her facial expression, she knew it.

Chance's manic laughter radiated all around, echoing in my head, mocking my clumsy movement.

The blurry figures dotting the sky circled us before dropping straight down and landing behind us.

Beasts.

His beasts.

They were smaller than dragons, but deadly just the same. Chance's Tarragon.

"Hello, Maker." They spoke as one, fangs protruding from their decrepit mouths.

Four more landed next to the existing six. All looked at me with malice in their eyes. As one, they stood to their full height, and my stomach hollowed out. They were at least twenty feet tall with large taloned hands, barbed tails, and scales that couldn't be burnt.

"Tate, run!" Shae shouted as she jumped in front of me, wielding her ice into a protective barrier. The Tarragon began charging, and Shae thickened the wall of solid ice, blocking their path, and then sent it a hundred feet up in the air.

My feet pounded the glass shards, loose rocks, and rubble as I raced through the city to the only exit—the one leading directly to Chance.

I glanced behind me to see Shae charging after me, icing the ground behind her. The Tarragon roared as one, and several began to fly. Some attempted to climb the ice but fell, even using their talons as ice picks. Two breached the wall and came soaring toward us.

"RUN!" Shae commanded bolts of ice to pour from the sky, striking the beasts soaring toward us. A few spears hit true, and the creatures roared at impact; one fell.

I turned my focus ahead just as my feet hit brown grass. I climbed the hill, falling once, and used my hands to lunge forward. Shae was directly behind me, shoving me forward as she iced the ground we'd just covered. More spears of ice poured from the sky, striking the ground behind us. A roar followed; she hit another one of the Tarragon.

We breached the top of the hill, and any air left in my tired lungs fled. Before us was a valley, one I didn't recognize, and in it were rows upon rows of gurneys. Each one held a body, varying in size and age.

"What in blood is happening?" I asked.

Shae's back went rigid next to me. Her eyes emptied as devastation tore across her face.

"This is my army," Chance shouted as he jumped from the side and landed in front of us in a crouch. Red bolts of static power coiled across his body and danced across his chest. The lightning covered the ground, webbing out toward us. "What do you think?"

"You've lost your mind!" I shouted as I stormed closer to him.

He smiled, revealing his fangs. "Or perhaps, I've finally found it."

"Chance, this is not who you are," Shae spoke calmly as she formed another wall of ice behind us, sending it spearing up hundreds of feet in the air to block the Tarragon climbing the hill behind us. Tiny balls of ice rolled down her forehead and cheeks.

"You're wrong. This is who I am. Who I was meant to be. I *am* power. Just like you, Shae. I changed; you've changed." He nodded to the ice forming behind Shae, to the icicles pouring from the sky behind us, pelting his creatures.

"And those poor people? What of them? Did they have a choice?" I challenged, fists balled at my sides.

"Did I have a choice? Did Shae? When *you* made us into these powerful beings, did you ask us first? No. What about the Tarragon? Again, the answer is *no*."

"What are you talking about? I never made you—"

"Oh, but you did." He tsked as he strode closer to me.

I eyed the gurneys below, noting the fangs protruding from the mouths of some. Vampires. He was using the Glenn's own citizens for his twisted army. I looked closer, sure enough, the guara's black and blue graced the bodies of countless figures resting on the gurneys. Others wore traditional clothes, several sporting the style of the human realm.

Countless lives stolen.

"What have you done?" The accusation left my lips at the same time rage erupted from within. I knelt and picked up a loose iron bar, likely from what was once a glorious, even if ugly, building in the Glenn. The rust-covered bar was in my hand as I took three daring steps toward Chance, ignoring Shae's cries for my patience.

Chance's nostrils flared, and from just a few mere feet away, I could *feel* the power rolling off him in waves of barely restrained energy.

"I've won. That's what." His fists flexed, and bolts of red lightning shot out haphazardly, tearing at the already dead grass.

"No." I shook my head, hand tightening on the bar. "You've lost *everything,* Chance. You lost it ALL."

He swallowed, almost as if recognizing the destruction his insanity wrought, but then he snarled, his righteous warpath assured.

"Chance." I forced my voice to remain even. "You've lost the Glenn. Any of your citizens that you thought you ruled over are *dead*. Look at what you've done!"

His eyes glossed over as he looked behind me. The ground shook, and I heard the snarls of his beasts not far behind.

"Shit." Shae pivoted, facing behind us as she no doubt unleashed her flurries of power upon the fanged creatures once more.

Chance smiled, sadly at first and then wildly as he threw his hands to the sky and called down lightning that struck his fingers and then fed back up into the sky. He pivoted, spinning in a circle, and surveyed the bodies, the destroyed city, the bones, the rubble, and the hundreds of corpses.

"Yes, look at it. It's beautiful. Each body on a gurney *is* my soldier. And I'm just getting started." As he finished speaking, the bolts flared once more and then vanished.

A melody began weaving through the air. And unlike before, where it was soft and comforting, this was an eerie version of a Winter Solstice song I'd once loved—a warning, a foreboding of what may come.

The air pulsed and flared, turning my entire vision white before it settled, and this time, we faced the cornerstones of the veil. Chance strode proudly to the closest pillar; red lightning zapped the grass and dirt beneath his feet. Behind us lay the Glenn's city ruins. Ahead was the veil: the magical wall that separated the vampire world from the human one.

"Chance. You can't," Shae panted.

The Tarragon stood in a crouch next to Chance, to our side, and behind us. Shae readied another icicle in her palm and then handed me one. My hand jolted from the cold, and with it the realization that I no longer had my iron bar—without the icicle, I was weaponless.

My grip tightened, slipped, and then secured the ice wand.

The Tarragon roared, black saliva flying from their mouths. One of them took a proud step closer to Chance. It was the biggest one and seemed the most self-assured—its eyes boasted an edgy intelligence that the other beasts didn't possess.

"I often wondered, why have the veil? We're superior to humans.

They're beneath us—our food source. It's time they serve us as nature intended."

"STOP!" Shae shouted, and a series of icicles flew out and impaled the ground surrounding the cornerstone, blocking Chance from it.

"Really, Shae? You always did choose *her*." He looked at me and spat.

"This isn't right. Leave the veil, Chance." My voice filled with righteous indignation. The humans had always been protected under the No-Kill Law—a law Chance himself had once upheld. Now he wanted to tear the wall down? Destroy the veil and wreak his manic havoc on the human realm?

No.

I stepped closer to Chance, following Shae's lead, and ignored the increased snarling at my back. The melody weaving all around hit an unnatural note, and it started over in a minor key. Wrongness seeped from each note, from the grass, from Chance, from this whole blood-forsaken place.

"I could leave it...but where's the fun in that?" He laughed and then sent a flurry of bolts toward us. I lunged to the left, and Shae manifested a shield around us. Chance turned, ignoring us and struck the cornerstone with his power. He called it down from the sky, and it hit him before he directed it into the stone itself.

The ground shook.

The sky blackened.

The Tarragon hooped and hollered, dancing as they made keening sounds of joy.

The stone shuddered and then split open, and blood began to pour from it, saturating the dry earth. Like a geyser, it erupted, and blood no longer streamed from it, but exploded.

Chance laughed.

A clock ticked.

The world spun, and then Shae dropped the shield and sent a wave of ice out at Chance. In his crazed state, he didn't notice the streams of frozen water that struck the static dancing across his core. He screamed and then dropped to his knees, jolting. The Tarragon howled and then charged, claws tearing into the ground as they bounded toward us across the small distance. Shae called down rods of ice to strike them as she grabbed my hand, leading me toward the now disintegrating veil.

Slowly, the translucent curtain of power flickered and faded, evaporating into nothing, leaving the human realm completely vulnerable. Their buildings stood proud, cars dotted their highways, planes flew in their skies. Pedestrians strolled down the city streets, unaware of the imminent threat.

Chance roared behind us, and we darted through the now vanishing veil into the human realm. The gnashing of teeth was just at our heels. I turned and stabbed a tarragon in the head with the ice. It didn't so much as penetrate, but it distracted it long enough for Shae to render a sled of ice beneath us and send us hurtling down the hill toward the human city.

The world pulsed as the new minor note struck, and a *gong* sounded. A door appeared at the bottom of the hill. It flashed and then released inky black waves of energy.

Using ice to direct us, Shae willed us toward the door.

"YOU CAN'T ESCAPE ME! I AM YOUR FUTURE!" Chance roared from behind.

Our sled hit the door, and Shae and I went tumbling through the entrance on impact. We were held in the embrace of the dark waves of energy. Behind us, the Tarragon charged the door but impacted a solid wall and were not allowed to follow as we drifted amongst the nothingness. The webs and tendrils of darkness.

The future foreseen is not set,
The events witnessed were imagined,
One possible, plausible, bet,
As to what may be predestined.

The words swirled around us and then abruptly ended as Shae's hand reached for mine, and we found ourselves back in the cabin. Alone.

The boys were gone.

I looked at Shae and then back to the door. The oily black waves vanished, and the door became translucent once more. The portal was closed, and Chance and Aether were gone—stuck in the vortex of hell.

CHAPTER 11
AETHER

"**A**ETHER! Who the fuck do you think you are?" Chance demanded, jumping off the couch and rushing me once more.

"I'm the male whose bonded was just sucked into a blood-forsaken portal, and you're the asshole in my way!" I growled as I sent a punch flying in his direction. He evaded again and counter struck, a punch that I too sidestepped while I kicked his feet out from under him.

I dropped to pin him, but he rolled and was on his feet once more, swinging for me. I accepted his impact and wrapped my arms around his waist, dragging him with me to the ground, grappling for power.

Tate was gone. Taken with Shae into the portal. My beloved was taken from me.

The door flared, and waves of ink poured across the ground. I shoved Chance and used my weight to pin him down. With a right hook, I caught his left eye. Then his lip. I cocked my arm back, prepared to strike once more, when he kneed my groin. I inhaled sharply at the pain, but refused to slacken my grip on him.

The waves of darkness moved to coat his arm and then my leg. Still, I refused to budge, determined to strangle him.

The darkness tightened around my body like a vice and then, with an extreme force, yanked me into the doorway with Chance.

We were spinning and twisting in clouds of black energy that sparked and sizzled as the portal's power tore Chance and I apart. I allowed its energy to inspect me, coat my features, and then send me tumbling head over heels at an immaterial space.

Bright light enveloped me, and my knees impacted stone. I blinked. I was in a jail cell. My hands pressed against the cold stone floor. Grime met my fingertips as the distinct scent of mildew filled my nostrils. I glanced up and noted a bound figure in the corner, chained and adorned in rags composed of a familiar black material that was wholly bloodied.

"Where the fuck did you take me?!" Chance shouted from beside me.

My body tensed as I prepared for his impact, but then the figure in the corner coughed several times, and a new voice began to hum a melody that echoed throughout the dungeon's cell. Chance's motion ceased.

Following Chance's gaze, I looked behind me, through the bars, to a short female who approached the cell, a tray in her hands. She hummed a contented melody and wore a plain pink dress with a white apron. Something triggered my memory. I'd seen her before...

"You," Chance said breathlessly as he stormed the iron bars.

The female ignored him, as if we were non-existent, and instead lowered herself to shove the tray underneath the bars.

"Here you go. I'm truly so sorry it came to...this." Her voice trailed off as sympathy lit her features.

The crumpled, broken figure in the corner rolled over so he faced the young female servant. He coughed, and blood spurted from his freshly busted lip that complemented the scar cutting through the right side of his face.

My breath stilled in my lungs as I stared at...myself.

"What type of fuckery is this?!" Chance demanded, shock and rage mixing in his eyes before they landed on the servant girl and instantly softened.

"Tha-thank you," the other version of me spoke, his speech as broken as his body appeared.

Iron prongs wrapped around his feet, and his hands were manacled with what appeared to be magic-laced metal bands, runes carved into each one.

"Of course. It's literally the least I could do. I just wish I could've stopped her. Stopped this. Just—I failed you both, and I'm truly sorry." She sniffed and then jolted at the sound of a door grating open at the end of the hall.

Chance snarled next to me, leaning into the bars and attempting to peer down the hallway. His left hand instinctively pulsed, as if calling his power, but nothing happened.

The other me crawled toward the tray and picked up a piece of bread, hand shaking violently. "P-please tell, tell me-e that sh-she's okay."

Who? Blood, tell me he's not referring to Tate?

Panic raced through my veins, and I squatted next to the broken, disfigured version of myself. "Where is she?" I growled.

But the other me merely lifted his quaking hand to his split, dried lips and attempted to eat the crumbling bread.

"She's no better than before. But I haven't given up. I promise. I'm working on it." The servant stood abruptly and squared her shoulders as two guards approached.

Chance reached through the bars for the girl, only for his fingers to brush the hem of her cape and fall short.

"The Queen Mother wants to see you. Now," one guard spoke, roughly grabbing her left arm in his hand.

She tugged on it lightly, and his grip only tightened along with the snarl across his face.

"LEAVE HER!" Chance shouted, but again no one responded.

"Why? I've done nothing!" the girl shouted, struggling against the guard's grip. She gained an inch only for the other guard to grab her right arm and begin dragging her away.

"STOP!" Chance shouted, banging against the bars loudly, slamming his body into them.

The girl looked over her shoulder and latched her eyes onto Chance. "Help me, please. Help me save them."

With that, the guards shoved her through the large door at the end of the hall and sealed the heavy iron door shut, locking it behind them.

"NO!" Chance shouted, slamming his body against the cell's bars again and again.

"It-it's no use." The broken version of me quivered. I leaned in closer to peer into my own disfigured face.

"Where's Tate?"

My own eyes peered back at me, black and full of sorrow.

"Save her," he spoke clearly before falling limp.

No! I reached down and gripped his broken tunic, shaking his unresponsive body.

Nothing.

"We need to get out of here," I spoke, squaring off against the bars.

"How?" Chance gritted out.

I loathed the word I spoke next. "Together."

Chance snarled at me, took a step closer with balled fists, but then froze. His eyes darted down the dungeon's hallway toward the locked door at the end and then back to me. "Fine."

I swallowed back the bile and hate racing through my gut and instead focused on the one person who mattered: Tate. We had to find her.

"On the count of three." I nodded to the iron bars and took a step back. Chance nodded.

"One." I inhaled.

"Two." I leaned forward.

"Three." I ran toward the bars, Chance following my lead. We hit them together, but they didn't give. The reverb sent us careening back into the cell's brick walls.

I expected to hit mortar, for pain to erupt, but instead we kept falling through the mirage of stone until we landed on a pink carpet on the other side.

I stood abruptly, shaking my head, and braced for an attack. We were in a grand throne room. All around were vases holding rose gold flowers, roses, and lilies. The floor was a pink and gold marble with a long pink rug running down the center. Tall columns of white stone with pink flecks stood twenty feet or taller to a vaulted ceiling. And there, at the end of the rug, stood a tall, high-back throne with a small chair next to it. Each was occupied.

It couldn't be, could it? My breath lodged in my throat as I paced forward, ignoring Chance, who seemed to be searching for something, or likely someone, the servant girl.

My feet ate at the carpet until I was close enough to confirm my suspicion. There on the throne sat a goddess with pink-tipped blonde hair and mahogany eyes. She was clothed in an ornate pink gown that complemented the heavy crown she wore. She tilted her glorious head back and laughed at something the dark-haired male next to her said. I ground my teeth. I recognized him too, but couldn't recall why or how. The harder I tried, the more the pain in my head increased.

Fuck this whole place.

Tate adjusted in her seat, moving a bit robotically, and leaned in closer to the male who caressed her forearm as if she were *his.*

I snarled as I stormed the stage, only to be suspended mid-step.

The throne room doors burst open, and guards entered, dragging the servant girl forward. Blood dripped from a gash on her head and stained her light pink dress.

Chance bounded toward her only to find himself also stuck, unable to move his feet even an inch.

I fought against my invisible restraints and shouted in frustration, but Tate appeared unfazed.

Her normally shrewd mahogany eyes were empty as they looked at the girl. She moved again in her seat, her head jerking in an uncontrolled motion, twitching almost, before settling in a new position.

"Your majesty, the traitor has been located. We believe *she* is why he's alive still." The guards threw the girl on the floor, and she skirted across the carpet until her motion stopped a few feet from Tate's throne.

Tate glared at her with vacant eyes as her head swiveled, and her limbs moved unnaturally. Something was very, very wrong.

"I see. You realize you've been keeping him alive, which means you've been keeping me weak," Tate spoke, but her voice was not her own.

"Tate! REMEMBER!" the girl shouted, tears springing from her eyes. "This isn't you!"

The male on the throne next to Tate stood, took several steps down to the girl, and struck her with the back of his hand. "You do not speak to the QUEEN!"

"NO!" Chance roared from behind, and this time, he was allowed to move forward until he was parallel with me, mere feet away from the girl in front of the throne, from my Tate. I lurched, attempting to move, but found my feet still glued securely to their spot by an unknown force.

A melody began to weave throughout the room, played by an orchestra I couldn't locate. The tune played with unnerving precision. It was a Winter Solstice love ballad, but in the current setting, it felt wrong, like a mockery. Each note, each verse, ridiculed the situation and then repeated it louder and louder.

The dark-haired male kicked the servant girl and then ran a hand through his hair. He looked expectantly up at Tate.

Her face held a brief note of agony that quickly smoothed over with indifference.

"Very well. You shall now be sentenced to death." Tate's voice floated through the room; her voice, but not hers—the inflection was all wrong.

"Tate!" I shouted. She didn't so much as flinch.

I fought the force holding me at bay as the guards retrieved the girl once more and began to drag her from the room, ignoring her cries.

"STOP!" Chance shouted, swiping pointlessly at the air.

"Wait," Tate's voice whispered.

I looked at her, hope rising in my chest. Perhaps she was still there.

"Do it here," she commanded before loosening a foreign laugh as her head jerked oddly.

"NO! Tate!" I screamed, but again, it fell on deaf ears.

The guards pulled out a post from the corner of the room and began to secure the girl's hands to bindings at the top.

The melody hit new notes, wrong notes.

I squinted at Tate and spotted it then: strings. Hard to see, but present just the same. I followed the clear strands up until I noted a balcony above the throne, a small alcove that held a cruel figure smiling with ruby red lips and red eyes. She held two different sticks that connected to the strings. She moved them one way, and Tate jolted with them, following her lead. The figure spoke, and then Tate's lips moved, "Kill her here."

Fuck that. Tate wasn't someone's puppet.

A loud ticking sounded above, and the notes hit a disturbing minor key as the guards finished securing the servant girl's hands to the post.

"Chance, listen to me." I turned my livid eyes to him. "This place is a living hell, but it's not real. That's not Tate. And that girl, whoever she is, isn't real either. No more than the fake me down in the dungeons was. The clock's started, which means we need to solve this test. I think we need to kill the puppet master up there," I spoke slowly, willing Chance's wild eyes to focus and understand the truth in what I said.

"I can't leave her," he whispered as he gazed at the whimpering girl.

One of the guards near her withdrew a large sword.

"Chance, we have to—"

"No! You kill the puppet master. I'm saving her."

I heaved. Arguing with him was pointless. This whole fucking thing was a nightmare.

With the first gong, the foreign force on my legs vanished, and I sprinted—past my injured Tate, the love of my life. Past the acidic male next to her. I ran to the stairs in the far corner and took them two at a time. I breached the balcony's surface and spotted the female manipulating Tate, her back to me.

Down below, the guards screamed as Chance relieved one guard of his sword and then the other of his head before pivoting once more and slicing through the first guard.

The puppeteer looked over her shoulder and sneered at me.

"Frightened by what you see?" She smiled coolly. "Well, good. You should be."

With that, she yanked on the strings dramatically and tugged Tate upward, sending her body arching through the air until she landed in front of me. This time, Tate brandished a sword and staggered toward me with unnatural movements.

"This isn't real!" I screamed, reminding myself of the truth.

The figure behind Tate smirked. "Oh, but it *could* be. This is a glimpse at what may occur."

Tate lurched forward, the sword pointed at me.

"I'm not fighting her!" I shouted, but even as I spoke, Tate advanced once more.

"Fight her or don't, either way you die." The figure behind Tate laughed, her voice harmonizing with the putrid noise blaring throughout the throne room.

The energy in the room rippled and then thrummed. A door flashed, appearing behind Tate and to the side of the maddening puppeteer.

I glanced down to see Chance, holding the servant girl, her lips whispering something in his ear.

"THE DOOR!" I shouted, and he glanced up at me before refocusing on the female he held.

Fuck it, I tried. Tate swung again, wavering on legs that stepped awkwardly—likely the manipulating female didn't understand how Tate had learned to accommodate having one leg shorter than the other her entire life. That and she was forcing my bonded to move in a way that was unnatural and went against her very being.

Tate's blade arched toward me, and I ducked, rolling to the side before springing forward and gripping the hilt of the sword. Tate's eyes flared, and something like recognition shown there. For the briefest moment, she softened, *she* returned, but then the puppeteer snarled and tugged on the strings, and Tate's grip tightened on the sword's handle once more.

The gong sounded for the fifth time, and the cacophony hit its final pass through the chorus I'd once sung cheerfully as a boy.

I tore the sword from Tate's grip, wincing as she cried out in pain at the unnatural angle her wrist turned. With a swift swipe, I sliced the strings from above her head, and she fell to the ground in a lifeless heap. The female behind her screamed, revealing fangs and pointed ears. She dropped to the wooden rods before throwing her mental power at me in a wave of glittering energy.

I pivoted to avoid the blast but wasn't fast enough as her power cascaded over my body and hindered me motionless.

It squeezed my heart, and claws sank into my mind and soul.

Tate looked up at me with teary eyes. "I'm so sorry."

I wanted to assure her this wasn't her fault. I wanted to comfort her, pick her up. But this wasn't real. None of it was.

A flash occurred and Chance stood behind the female. He looked at the door, then at me. With a quick snarl, he smacked the female on the head, rendering her unconscious, and then tore across the floor toward the now flickering door.

The hold on me disappeared and I sprang to my feet. The eleventh gong sounded, and the portal shook in an unstable tremble.

Tate lay unconscious on the ground.

"I'm going to fix this," I whispered and then forced myself toward the portal that led to the real Tate, to my mate.

At the twelfth gong, my feet crossed the doorframe, and I was pulled into the void.

My body tumbled through dark waves of power that wrapped

around me and squeezed. A certain feeling, a foreboding, crept through my conscience before a light appeared ahead.

I swam for it, pushing against the thick matter coiling around my body. I kicked and scooped through the inky nothingness, the raw energy, until my fingertips breached the light's circumference, and then my entire body thudded against rough wooden planks.

I blinked several times before shoving up from the wood.

Tate.

I searched the room and relief washed over me, loosening muscles and releasing a breath I'd held captive, when I spotted her sweet form rushing toward me.

She was all right.

We were all right.

CHAPTER 12
TATE

"**T**ATE! Thank blood," Aether's voice broke as he pulled me into a hug, tears dripping from his eyes.

"Aether," I murmured into his chest as I snuggled into his tight embrace. "It's okay."

What had he gone through? This strong male rarely cried, and for him to be this shaken?

The Wish World was a malicious place.

"You're all right. I didn't abandon you." His shoulder shook for a moment, and he released a long, tight breath, as I sank into his touch, offering the comfort of my body.

"I'm okay. You never abandoned me. I got pulled into a portal and well...we're all together now."

At that, he stiffened and surveyed the room. Chance stood near the fireplace, staring at the flickering flames with a haunted despair. Shae watched Chance sadly, a few feet away, near the tree, no doubt reliving what we experienced. I, too, watched Chance with a certain sadness and concern at the vision Shae and I shared. The potential future reality.

Shae's eyes locked onto mine, and she nodded once. We'd

discussed this; she'd try to save him, to keep him from rage and despair.

That future could never come to pass.

This world was cruel, preying on the emotions of its wishers in an attempt to break them, but it only served to strengthen our resolve.

A melody began to pour through the cabin, and the tree's lights flared once, highlighting three new ornaments: three doors.

One old, one looking fresh, and one that appeared futuristic.

The three large doorframes in the room flared and then slid together, forming one, before thrumming together. Aether pulled me closer to him as he stepped away from the shaking door. Energy vibrated from it, and then in a flash, it vanished, leaving three sparkling runes floating midair, one for each door.

The scent of baked chocolate filled the cabin, and four mugs of steaming blood cocoa appeared next to a plate of dragon-shaped cookies.

Runes appeared on the main cabin's exterior door's threshold. They flared and sparked, and then for the first time since we got here, the door became transparent, revealing a study I recognized intimately, Shae's home. A figure stood on the other side of the door, staring at the fireplace and chewing on her fingernails: Nora.

Shae stiffened and paced to the door, then froze. She rushed back to me and tore me from Aether's embrace, pulling me into a bear hug. I held her bony body in my arms and squeezed tightly.

"I'll see you again. Promise me, Shae, promise me this won't be the last time I see you," I whispered, swallowing thick emotion.

"I promise." She squeezed once more and then released me. With a sad smile, she nodded once and then turned to Aether. "Take care of her."

"Always."

She quirked a judgmental brow and then turned to Chance. "Let's go, bud."

Chance clenched his jaw but paced past us, shoulder bumping Aether on his way, before he strode through the door. With a final wave, Shae followed Chance through. It flared brightly, and then the wooden grain appeared once more.

"Well…" I started, unsure of what to do next.

The melody in the cabin softened, my favorite Winter Solstice song, simple and soothing. The tree's lights dimmed and twinkled. The fire crackled behind us, and Aether wrapped his arms around me from behind, leaning in to nuzzle my neck.

I savored this moment.

It was just us.

My heart ached from saying goodbye to Shae, but I meant what I told her. I'd see her again. And soon.

As if sensing my sadness even without our active bond, Aether began stroking my arms as he held me.

The exterior door rumbled and then flashed, revealing a familiar pebbled beach with a dark blue sea beyond.

It was time.

I looked up to Aether, who simply smiled.

"The sooner we leave here, the sooner we can get our family back," he spoke as he released me and offered his hand instead.

"Right. Then it's time." I took his hand in mine and followed him toward the portal.

With a final glance at the fire, all four stockings, and the tree with its new ornaments, I turned and, together, we took a step through the doorway.

Energy wrapped around my body and pulled me into a sparkling vortex. Crystals floated by us and all around us.

Each one hummed a melody.

Each one held a memory.

One showed Shae and I as kids, sledding down a hill, laughing uncontrollably.

Another showed Aether as a boy, sitting by a tree, gift in hand. I reached for that crystal, but it vanished before I could reach it, and I began moving at lightning speed through memory after memory.

Presents, gifts, Fletch, Irene, Chance, Shae, and Aether…

After a dizzying moment, the motion stilled, and my surroundings began to solidify. The distant sound of crashing waves, lapping water, and a gentle breeze tickled my ears.

I spotted small pebbles beneath my feet, faded but becoming more vibrant, tangible, with each passing moment.

You've been given a gift, oh favored one. Few visit the Wish World, and even fewer return with their sanity intact. Go now in peace.

An ethereal voice boomed before vanishing and allowing my surroundings to fully materialize.

I stood on the pebbled beach with Aether a few feet to my side. He looked at me, deep emotion filling his eyes.

The distant waves crashed, and I inhaled the salty scent of the sea.

"This is real," I murmured.

He walked back to me, tipped up my chin, and lowered his lips to where they were a mere breath away.

"This is real," he confirmed and then kissed me, taking my lips tenderly in his.

I melted into his arms for a moment, savoring the flavor that was truly his. He pulled back and then rested his forehead against mine.

Real, he assured me through our bond.

We were back in Mydant.

Back in our reality.

We may have survived the Wish World, but the future held many challenges, and the first one hovered just above my head, an icon and threat to our existence here.

A sign of the impending Challenging.

Without looking up or drawing his attention to *it*, I simply vowed to myself: we'd make it out of here, too.

NEED to know what happens next? Start the Untish Series on Kindle Unlimited and READ HERE!

Another Note from the Author

Thank you for indulging this holiday-inspired novella. I hope you thoroughly enjoyed tumbling through portals with our beloved cast of morally grey characters.

If you haven't read FANGS OF FATE, the very first book in the Untish Series, please enjoy this sneak peek!

FANGS OF FATE

REBECCA PARCHA

Untish Series Book One

CHAPTER ONE: TATE

The heat from the flames was getting closer. I needed to leave. He laid there, pinned against the floor by my body, my wrist at his throat. I dug the tip of my thumb in, pricking his skin. Blood bloomed where I squeezed. I leaned down and licked it up. It tasted remarkably good for a spoiled bag of blood like this man.

Ten innocents. He killed ten kids when he burned down the last apartment complex. Five of those children belonged to a foster family. He was an abomination to mankind and any death would be too kind for him.

His eyes were fully dilated, fear filled the air. I could taste it, a symphony to the iron on my tongue. He whimpered and I knew he'd beg for his life if I released enough pressure from his throat. I wouldn't though. I smiled icily. Bending over, I brushed my lips next to his ear, slowly exhaling.

"Judith. Amy. Kyle. Roy. Trever. Nancy." The names of the children he murdered. The ones he killed in cold blood. He shuddered and squirmed, trying to break free.

"Claire. Benny. Natalie. Hannah." I looked into his eyes—a window to a dark soul. "You took their lives. Consider this justice."

I lowered my mouth to his jugular and then clamped down. My fangs sank in slowly, lengthening the painful puncture. He screamed and it competed with the sound of the flames in the next room. The building would crumble, and his body would be the only one in the rubble. I had sounded the alarm and screamed 'fire' when the flames were but mere sparks.

The building was practically empty to begin with. He lived in a dump. The complex likely violated every regulation code there was, and anyone here was likely a convict and doped up on drugs like this bag of shit. I pulled deeply and filled my throat with his blood. It had been too long since I'd last fed. Feeding has always felt a bit at odds with my personality. In childhood, it had been rainbows and pink everything. *Then*, I'd had the warm embrace of my mother, the shelter of a safe home, and no concern as to whose blood I'd need to consume next. I was young. Now, all the warm safety of my childhood had been stripped, leaving me to deal with the steel of the world. Now, I was both predator and prey.

Feeding was what my nature demanded. And grotesque as I once saw it, it felt right. Especially when I was feasting from a degenerate like the man beneath me. I needed to release him. I could start to feel the heat creeping up from below. This room would be engulfed in flames soon. I couldn't drain his life force—it was against the rules of the Glenn. One more draw, then I'd release him and leave him to burn alive.

Images of those tiny corpses filled my mind. He had left them to burn, to die. He had been their foster dad and *he* had started the fire and left. He was a vile man. The pictures from Tim's computer wouldn't soon disappear. I still saw them when I laid awake at night. The small, charred teddy bear beside the body of an innocent soul—a mark that would forever scar my heart. They were human, I knew this.

I shouldn't care. I wasn't *supposed* to care. Yet, some part of my DNA couldn't leave it alone—I couldn't feed from humans if I didn't think they deserved it. It would be a fatal flaw had I not found a route around my conscience four years ago when I completed my turn. I was sixteen then; like all vampires, it was time to either transition or choose to live the life of a human...forever. Naturally, I chose the longer existence. My first mistake.

I drew again and began to withdraw but the flow down my throat was too sweet, it beckoned me further.

Sweat began to drip down my back, my forehead. Warm, very warm. The flames would be visible any minute.

Fire was fatal for my kind—a similarity we shared with humans. I should leave, should have already left, as I have no intention of going up in flames with him. But...the sweet iron liquid called to me. One more draw, just a *little* more. The cherry note to his blood was intoxicating.

I had been overfeeding lately; the past month I'd had an increase in both hunger and vengeance. It made sense. Or at least I believed so, given the date. One year ago today, my mother was taken from me. There would be no justice for her.

I could feel his body go limp beneath me. *Crack!* The sound of embers, of wood being swallowed whole by flames climbing the walls. Time was up. Closing my eyes, I drank. I pulled. I swallowed. His blood was almost gone, just a few drops remained. Two more drags and there was hardly anything left. But...I couldn't stop. The high from draining took over. My head swam, and adrenaline swallowed my senses. Power filled my veins; I squeezed his throat tighter and heard a *snap*, distantly aware that his jaw was no longer pressed against my cheek, that he made no other noises. He was gone. I pulled again, but this time no blood came. I had emptied him.

My energy doubled, strength flooding my system, and a comforting warmth flowed through my veins. My limbs tingled and my head felt light. There really wasn't anything like a blood-drain high.

Retracting my fangs from his throat, I let him fall to the floor in an unnatural heap. The room was on fire. I looked toward where the window was and only saw a wall of flames.

I could have just made a fatal mistake. I stood, angling my body to where I knew the window was. Blood help me. With a deep breath, I lunged through the flames, bright orange and hints of blue filled my vision. Heat swallowed me with intensity and drew the breath from my lungs.

I broke free from the fire and was falling in the crisp night air from the second story. I landed on the ground twenty feet below and tumbled. The glamour may hide my bone discrepancy, but gravity couldn't be fooled.

Deep breath in, steady.

Slowly, I rose from a crouch and shook out my legs. The old pain returned, but I blocked it out—easier to do on a blood-high. My skin itched but didn't hurt. Odd considering my contact with the flames.

Sirens sounded remarkably close, but no first responders. *Yet*. I rose from my crouched position and set into a jog, slow at first to allow my body time to recover from the trauma of the impact. I ran around the block, past the chain-link fence, down an alley, and then up another. After thirty minutes I approached my apartment. If I was ever thankful for my version of jogging, which rivaled most human athletes, it was in times like these. The high from feeding was still present, my head still abuzz.

The fire in my chest had been ignited.

Want to continue reading? Fangs of Fate is now available on Kindle Unlimited!

READ NOW!

THE UNTISH SERIES CONTINUES

Thank you for reading *Untish Wishes*. Tate's story continues in the third installment of the *Untish Series*, **coming soon!** If you haven't yet read **Fangs of Fate** and **Daughter of Destiny**, now is the perfect time to sink your fangs in!

"There's no world in which I exist and you don't"

Read Fangs of Fate now!

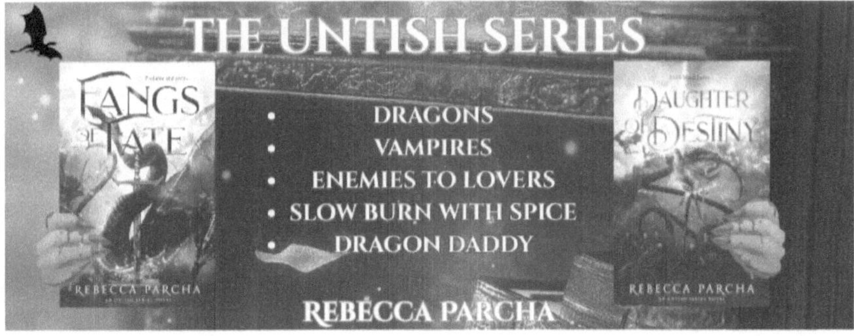

FANGS OF FATE

New to the series? Be sure to read *FANGS OF FATE*, book one in the *Untish Series*!

I am vengeance. Tate Aaralyn, a lone vampire vigilante who strikes fear into the hearts of monsters. My fangs puncture, and the flavor of iron-infused retribution drips down my throat when I exact justice.

Don't be like them. Don't succumb to bloodlust. Make the b*stards pay.

These rules have been my guide, leading me through life in the Glenn. And all had been flowing nicely until I met him...The male cloaked in secrets, wrapped in darkness, and holding the keys to my past and future: Aether.

Complex. Messy. Unexpected.

My whole world slipped into a tailspin of lies, betrayal, and secrets. As I'm forced into the guara with a male I loathe, yet somehow crave, I must not only untangle the truth of who I am, but also what I am.

I am the enforcer. Chance Dale, the vampire president's son holding a prestigious position as Dux in the guara. I command respect and provide results. I will not let the Glenn down.

Not as I hunt the traitor living among us. Not as dark magic's inky ways begin to seep into our villages. Not as vile beasts fill them.

Nothing will stop me from this path, not even her. Even if one thing is clear: the very enemy I hunt may be the one I love.

Fangs of Fate is an epic first-person dual-POV romantasy that will leave you breathless! Buckle up, grab a glass of bloodwine, and clear your calendar for this morally grey, intrigue-infused, and action-packed romance that stars vampires, dragon shifters, corruption, and deception—and secrets that can break even the strongest...

SINK YOUR 'FANGS' INTO THE UNTISH SERIES TODAY!

DAUGHTER OF DESTINY

MAGIC IS ITS OWN ENTITY. IT CAN BE AS RUTHLESS AS IT IS HELPFUL.

TATE AARALYN:

Dear blood, he was a dragon shifter. A male who was lethal in both forms, wielding *black* flames that were somehow light. And he wanted me... Claimed me. Desired me.

I never thought I'd find myself inside the Untish Embassy, masquerading as a Darkling... but then again, I never knew I was a rare vampire with a dragon shifting gift. And now, I'm haunted by my elusive past, while simultaneously hunted by my very own.

He says he can help me, wants to protect me, that it's *my* choice. But clothed in secrets, and leading a society that thrives on deceit, trusting Aether Brychan may be the one thing that gets me burned.

AETHER BRYCHAN:

She's exquisite. Everything I'm not. Everything I want to protect, honor, and worship... And they want to destroy her. Kill her.

Over my dead body.

I'm the embodiment of darkness, and I *will* protect my bonded from the monsters, scaled and not. Come what f*cking may.

CHANCE DALE:

My worst nightmare stalks on two feet; vile monsters crafted from dark magic.

With new power thrumming in my veins, the allure of it beckons, cleaving a way for me to control the dark magic. Only I can decide how far I'll go to defend those I'm sworn to protect.

Darkness and red warp everything. *Become* everything. Red lights the path to victory. Red strikes and destroys. This *RED* may just be my only saving grace...

In a world where half-truths and betrayals lurk in every shadow, three fates intertwine. A storm is coming—and when it breaks, only one will remain.

Daughter of Destiny is an epic fantasy centered in an urban, dragon-shifting world where the Chairs determine who you marry, and everyone must earn their place in this action-adventure romance! This paranormal romantasy boasts steamy spice with fated mates and banter that has readers devouring the pages, leaving them craving more. Step inside these morally grey characters' minds in this first-person, multi-POV, dark fantasy, where bloodwine is life and secrets are currency. But be forewarned, not everything is as it seems...

STEP INTO THE EMBASSY TODAY! NOW ON KINDLE UNLIMITED!

Acknowledgments

Thank *you* for embarking on this journey with me. *Untish Wishes* is an introductory novella to the *Untish Series*. While it's better enjoyed having read the first two books, beginning with *Fangs of Fate*, it's an independent novella that nods to book three. It was inspired by the holiday season and my love for the Untish world. I cannot begin to express my gratitude to you for taking a chance on me, a new author. I truly hope you've fallen in love with this world and these characters, who are very dear to my heart—even as they get darker and seem bleaker. How can there be light without darkness?

Thank you also to my amazing team, and to every single person who has helped make this dream a reality. Thank you to my husband, John, who has been unconditionally supportive. To all my friends and family who supported me, thank you for everything.

The story isn't finished! This is only the beginning for Tate, Chance, Aether, and Shae—along with all the other delicious morally grey characters.

SIGN UP FOR MY NEWSLETTER!

Stay in the know for all future releases, giveaways, and personal author updates!

SIGN UP HERE!

About the Author

I love all things fiction, specifically, fantasy. Add a little romance, or sometimes a whole heap, and you'll find my specialty: romantasy. As an avid reader and devourer of all things Fae, dragon, and magical, my work (as you may have guessed) is centered in that world. I love a strong female protagonist who defies the patriarchy while learning to love and trust.

I am one of the lucky ones; I married my high school sweetheart and am a mother of two adorable, rambunctious boys. As a Colorado native, I love the sunshine and crisp air while enjoying the outdoors with my guys...have I mentioned I'm outnumbered?

Stories have always held me captive—they are the air I breathe. It is my purest pleasure to share the tales that have been burning in my heart. To see a full list of my works, please visit my website: www.rebeccaparcha.com